Montgomery Lake High #2

When Darkness Tries to Hide

Written by Stacy A. Padula

Briley & Baxter Publications | Plymouth, Massachusetts

ISBN: 978-1-7350168-5-6

Book Design: Stacy O'Halloran

Dedicated to Debra Fredette

Meet the Characters

1st: Chris, Cathy, Jason, Chantal
2nd: Andy, Alyssa, Marc, Lisa
3rd: Courtney, Jon, Bobby, Marielle
4th: Bryan, Katherine, Leslie, Julianna

Chapter 1

Andy Rosetti woke up Thursday morning with a pounding heart. It was 5:33 a.m., and he did not have to get up for another hour. He glanced around his bedroom anxiously, wondering what had interrupted his sleep. Everything seemed at peace in his room, yet his heart was still pounding against his chest. Suddenly, the sound of heavy raindrops hitting his window caught his attention. Instantly, his bedroom became illuminated with bluish-white light. Within two seconds, crackling thunder erupted. Andy's heart began to pound more heavily. He took a deep breath and placed his head in his hands.

Andy had hated thunderstorms his entire life. The thought of his house getting struck by lightning terrorized him during every storm. He knew the storm was right above his house as lightning and thunder began erupting simultaneously. Burying his head beneath his pillow, Andy attempted to fall back to sleep. Three crashes of thunder later, he knew it was a lost cause.

Andy's cell phone began vibrating on his nightstand. He grabbed a hold of it, fearing the worst. Who would call him at 5:36 a.m.? He glanced at the caller ID and smiled: Lisa Ankerman.

"I figured the storm was keeping you awake," she greeted Andy as he answered the phone. "I thought you might like a distraction."

"You're good," Andy laughed, feeling his heartbeat slow down at the sound of his best friend's voice. "Woke you up, too, huh?"

"Yeah, we're going to have horrific weather today," Lisa replied. "My game's probably going to be cancelled."

"Jeff and I planned on watching you and Chantal cheer," Andy said, throwing the covers over his head. "If the game's cancelled, we should all hang out at my house or something."

"I made plans with Leslie for after the game," Lisa replied. "We'll keep our plans even if the game is cancelled."

"You sound like you're up to no good," Andy sang, knowing Lisa all too well.

Lisa laughed. "You can tag along if you'd like."

"Nah, not today," Andy replied quickly. "Chantal would kill me, and I can't make a habit of traveling that road. Once this week was enough."

"You're such a goody-goody," Lisa sighed, "but I love you for it."

"I'm Class President. I have *huge* responsibilities," Andy stated sarcastically. "Seriously, what would you guys do without me?"

"Oh yeah, I'm sure we'd fall apart," Lisa laughed. "All right, I'm going to hop in the shower before we lose the power. I'll see you at your locker, all right?"

"Sure thing," Andy replied. "Thanks for calling, Lis."

"Only because I love you that much," Lisa said. "Bye, Andy."

"Bye," Andy sang, as he hung up his cell phone. Lisa had been Andy's best friend since childhood. She knew him better than anyone else did. Andy smiled, grateful to have such a caring best friend. He glanced at his alarm clock, deciding it was time to start his day.

⸺✦⸺

Since September, Chris Dunkin had made a habit of praying each morning before school. He found the days he skipped prayer to be arduous. School, which used to be a giant social playground for Chris, had become a war zone.

Something amazing had happened to Chris, but no one wanted to hear about it. It seemed as if his classmates liked him better as a burnout than a competent jock. Chris never had trouble getting people's attention before. He had always been the center of everything social. No one had ever questioned his leading. Everyone had always followed him with ease, but now they were abrasive.

Whenever Chris had found out about a new drug circulating, a new bridge to jump off, or a new pit to party at, everyone had extolled him. Now that he had found something greater than all of the above, no one would listen to him. In the past month, kids at school had begun throwing strange glances in his direction. He knew it was the result of Jason's rumors.

Chris's childhood best friend, Jason Davids, was a punk. Quick-witted, articulate, and as charismatic as anyone could be, Jason was a harbinger of destruction. He could make people laugh like no one else, and everyone loved him for it. His words were as slick as black ice. He was usually high during five of the eight periods in a day, yet he pulled off A's in every class. To top it off, he dated one of the Kagelli twins, whom everyone wanted to get with. Jason knew how to work the system.

Chris and Jason had been best friends for ten years. Chris had never expected Jason to turn on him with such force. What grieved

Chris's heart was not the harm done to his reputation, his tainted image, or the strange way people were treating him. He couldn't have cared less about what people thought of him. What grieved his heart was that he knew where Jason was headed. *Pride goes before destruction, and a haughty spirit before a fall.* When Chris had read that in Proverbs, he knew God was ministering to him about Jason.

Getting on his knees at the end of his bed, Chris prayed, "Father, help. Despite what Jay is doing to me, I still love him like a brother. I want him to come to know You. He needs You. He needs to see that he is in darkness and that everything he is living for is futile. Please open his eyes. Please, whatever it takes, bring him to the end of himself."

⸻⚜⸻

In the backseat of his brother Luke's BMW, Jason Davids sat beside Marc Dunkin on his way to school. Marc was a senior at MLH and co-captain of the Varsity football team. He was Luke's wingman and Chris's cousin. The Davids and Dunkin families had been well-acquainted for years.

"Slow down, dude! The roads are slick," Marc exclaimed, patting Luke on the shoulder. "Your girlfriend is in the car," he added, referring to Missy Kent, the stunning blonde who was sitting shotgun.

"I know how to handle this baby," Luke replied, patting the dashboard. "I love this car."

Marc rolled his eyes. "No doubt my practice is going to be cancelled today. The field is probably mush by now. JV won't be able to play either."

"Your cousin is sick on the field," Luke stated, putting on his blinker to turn into the high school's parking lot. "No doubt he takes right after you."

"Yeah, except Marc never joined a cult," Jason stated dryly. "You have to talk to him about that."

Marc shrugged. "Whatever works for him. Honestly, I'm proud of Chris. My whole family is."

Jason rolled his eyes and glanced at the rain drizzling down his window.

⁓⬥⁓

"Hey Court, what's up?" Chris called, appearing at Courtney Angeletti's locker before homeroom.

"Not much!" Courtney replied, twirling around in recognition of her ex-boyfriend's deep voice.

Chris smiled. "Are you going to Alyssa's party tomorrow night?"

"Oh, please," Courtney rolled her eyes. "I can't believe she's going to risk having a party. After getting arrested at Jason's last month, I would think she'd be careful," she reasoned.

"Alyssa Kelly?" Chris laughed. "No, never. I've been friends with that girl for way too long to expect any sign of intelligence from her."

Courtney smiled. "Are you going?"

Chris laughed, "Uh, that would be a solid **no**."

"Good answer," she said and winked at her close friend. Over the summer, Courtney had broken up with her long-term boyfriend, Bryan Sartelli, to date Chris. She had done that because she wanted a taste of the rebellious lifestyle Chris led. Ironically, Chris had begun dating Courtney because he wanted an out from that same lifestyle. During their breakup, Chris had told Courtney his reasoning, and she had been shocked. Prior to their breakup, Courtney had been too wrapped up in herself to even realize Chris felt discontent. In dire need to feel accepted by the popular crowd of her freshman class, Courtney had flushed her values, morals, compassion, empathy, and consideration down the toilet. Alyssa Kelly and Cathy Kagelli had decided to take Courtney under their wings, and that had consumed her.

Chapter 2

"So, did you invite her?" Alyssa asked on the walk home from school later that afternoon with Cathy and Jason.

"Who?" Cathy shivered and glanced at Alyssa strangely.

"Julianna Camen!" Alyssa clarified, passing a lit cigarette to Cathy.

Cathy nodded, hesitantly taking the cigarette from Alyssa.

"Julianna Camen?!" Jason exclaimed, widening his cobalt blue eyes in disapproval. Julianna was his friend Jon Anderson's new girlfriend. Jon had begun dating her after his dramatic breakup with Alyssa at Jason's last party. As if that was not enough of a reason for Alyssa to resent Julianna, Julianna was best friends with Cathy's favorite enemy: Courtney Angeletti.

"I'm going to invite her to get ready with me for the party," Cathy replied nonchalantly.

"Why would you two be interested in hanging out with *her*?" Jason questioned the girls.

Alyssa shrugged. "To help her fit in better?" she suggested and turned towards Cathy.

"No," Cathy shook her head and rolled her eyes at Alyssa, "to get back at Courtney, Chantal, and Jon."

"For what?!" Jason exclaimed, glaring at his girlfriend. "Don't tell me you're still pissed off about what happened at my party? Chantal had nothing to do with that. Jon was just mad at Alyssa and threw Chantal's name into the mix to be a jerk."

"Shut up about that!" Cathy demanded, pushing Jason in the shoulder. "If Julianna becomes friends with us, she'll ditch them in a heartbeat. Maybe you'll get your friends back, too."

Jason glared at Cathy in disbelief. "You're terrible," he stated after a moment. He shook his head in disgust as he stalked off ahead of his girlfriend. He had begun to think that Cathy enjoyed playing with people's minds. Although he liked to tease his friends, Jason never intentionally wanted to hurt anyone. In fact, he just wanted everyone to have fun. He hated drama, hated mind games, and, more than anything, hated cigarette smoking. Even though a lot of his friends smoked, he had never expected his own girlfriend to join the bandwagon.

When he first met Cathy, he had been attracted to her dry sense of humor, quick wit, love of adventure, and physical appearance. After two years of dating her, he'd learned many of those qualities went hand in hand with the things he hated most about her.

Chapter 3

After arriving at Cathy's house, Alyssa, Jason, and Cathy had intended to spend a couple of hours planning out the details for Alyssa's Halloween party. However, the nasty thunderstorm that was ripping through neighboring towns and heading toward Montgomery had caught Alyssa's notoriously strict mother's attention.

"We just got here. We're safe. It's not even raining anymore," Alyssa spoke into Cathy's home phone while Cathy and Jason eyed her curiously. "Why?" Pause. "Seriously?" Pause. "Well if that happens, we can just go to the basement. Why do I have to come home?"

Cathy scowled. If Mrs. Kelly picked up Alyssa, it would put a huge damper on their party planning, considering that the event was only twenty-seven hours away. Mr. and Mrs. Kelly were taking Alyssa's brother John and his fiancé away for the weekend as an engagement present. Alyssa had told her parents she would spend the weekend at Cathy's—unbeknownst to Cathy's parents—creating the perfect opportunity to host a party inside her parentless home.

"Fine. I'll be ready," Alyssa huffed before hanging up the phone. "I hate my mother," she stated and placed the phone down on the counter. "She wants me home in case the thunderstorm that tore through Springfield makes its way here."

"It's supposed to," Jason said. "That's why every after-school sport was cancelled today."

Cathy rolled her eyes. "Are you serious? How are we supposed to plan your party? Over the phone?"

Alyssa shrugged. "I guess. Sorry. You know how my mom is. She said we could get hit with a supercell."

"A supercell? In Massachusetts?" Cathy questioned her in a mocking tone.

Alyssa shrugged again.

Cathy sighed. "Hopefully with Luke's help, we can contain the party to thirty people. Neither one of us can afford to get in trouble again."

"He'll make sure nothing gets out of hand," Jason assured her.

"Good!" Alyssa cried. "Oh, Cathy, can you hold onto these and bring them tomorrow night?" she asked while pulling a pack of cigarettes out of her pocketbook. "I'm afraid my parents will search my bag."

"Sure," Cathy replied and took the cigarettes from her.

Jason rolled his eyes. "Luke got those for Alyssa, not you."

"I know," Cathy said defensively.

"Oh, like you're not going smoke?" Jason retorted in a frustrated manner.

Cathy lowered her eyebrows. "I hate cigarettes. I only smoke when I want to upset you or my parents."

"I never thought in a million years that you would ever condone, let alone start, smoking," Jason stated angrily.

Cathy rolled her eyes. "I would never 'start' smoking. You're just mad that I gave up weed."

"No. I'm mad that you're acting insane!" Jason cried.

Cathy raised her eyebrows. "Insane?"

"*Insane*," Jason repeated.

"Uh, guys? Can you wait till I leave to start fighting?" Alyssa whined. "My mom will be here in five minutes."

Cathy glanced at Alyssa and then locked her eyes back on Jason. "You know what? I'm going outside to smoke right now, just to spite you."

"Why are you being such a @#%$?" Jason asked and threw his hands up in the air.

Alyssa scowled. "All you two do is fight," she muttered.

Cathy rolled her eyes and walked out the door to her back porch. She had absolutely no intention of smoking, but she needed to make Jason think she did. He no longer seemed to mind when she took Xanax or Klonopin, so smoking was one of the only things she could do—or pretend to do—to make him worry about her.

The sound of the kitchen door opening startled Cathy and pulled her away from her thoughts.

"I knew you weren't smoking," Alyssa said in an amused manner after she stepped outside. "You love to piss him off, don't you?"

Cathy smiled.

"Well, my mom's going to be here in a minute, so I just wanted to say bye. Good luck with Jay," Alyssa said and eyed Cathy precariously.

"Thanks. Call me later."

"Sure thing," Alyssa called as she walked towards the door.

After Alyssa disappeared inside, Cathy contemplated how long she should stay outside before contending with her boyfriend. Even though Jason had promised to get a handle on his Adderall abuse, his drug habits had not changed. He was still caught in an Adderall-weed cycle and still abusing Vicodin when he drank. Cathy had begun to wonder if he was being sincere when he promised to clean up his act or if he had merely told her what she wanted to hear.

A moment later, she walked inside and found Jason sitting in the living room, staring at his phone. When she entered the room, he did not glance in her direction. Knowing Jason could not stand discord, Cathy sat down beside him and waited for him to begin trying to make sense of her odd behavior.

Jason glanced to his left after a moment and glared at her. "I don't understand you anymore," he said calmly, although he looked annoyed. "It feels like you are doing everything you can to piss me off."

Cathy widened her eyes in an amused manner. "So, maybe I'm going insane?"

"It's not funny, Cathy. Don't turn this into a joke."

Cathy laughed. "I'm not. What if you're right? What if I'm really losing it?"

Jason scowled. "I have never seen someone's personality change as drastically as yours in a month."

"Oh, are you worried?" Cathy asked and smiled.

Jason threw his hands up in the air. "Why do you want me to be worried?"

Cathy smiled. "I already told you why."

"And I asked you to give me time to fix myself."

"I did, and nothing changed."

Jason groaned. "The K-pins are making you careless and rude. That's the only explanation I can come up with. You not on benzos would never smoke."

"I don't smoke," Cathy insisted and shook her head.

"You just did!"

"No, I didn't. Smell my hands," she said and put her fingers up to his nose. "I just pretended to do it to upset you."

Jason widened his blue eyes. "I don't even know how to take you anymore. If that's true, then that's just as effed up as you actually smoking."

Cathy flipped her hands in the air. "Well, what can I say? I'm really good at messing with your head."

"I don't know how to fix this," Jason said. "I'm making you go crazy, and I'm not in love with sociopath-Cathy."

"Yeah, well, I'm in love with sober-Jason," Cathy retorted. "Haven't seen that kid in a while."

"So, what are we doing then?" Jason asked with frustration in his voice.

"I'm just trying to cope with your issues," Cathy replied in an innocent tone and then lay down across his lap. "You've turned ninth grade into quite an adventure," she added and tugged on his shirt.

Jason rolled his eyes.

She sat up and straddled him. Planting her hands on his shoulders, she looked directly into his blue eyes. "At the end of the day, all I want is us," she said in her normal, sweet voice.

"Oh, hi, Cathy," Jason remarked sarcastically. "Did the demon that's been overruling you for the last two weeks finally let you speak?"

Cathy laughed. "We both need to chill out," she said. "Weed would probably help."

Jason raised his eyebrows. "*You* want to smoke?"

"If it will help us end this stupid, petty fight," Cathy replied. "I don't want to fight with you. I love you."

Jason eyed her strangely for a few seconds and then shrugged. "All right. We better hit it now before the storm gets here." He let out a heavy breath before standing up from the couch.

Cathy could tell by the bewildered expression on his face that she had successfully gotten in his head. She had perfected the art of pushing him to his near breaking point and then pulling him right back into her arms. All it ever took was a moment of acting like her normal self to fill him with hope that she was still the girl he loved.

Chapter 4

The scheduled JV football game had been postponed as a result of the severe storm warning issued across the county. Sitting on her queen-size bed, Chantal Kagelli bit her French-manicured fingernails. "I don't know what we can do." She shrugged and glanced at her boyfriend Andy. "I planned on cheering at the game."

"We can go to my house," Andy suggested. "We could call Chris and Marielle and see what they're up to. Maybe they'll want to hang out."

"Doesn't Chris have practice even though the game was cancelled?" Chantal asked, reaching toward her white wicker nightstand for the cordless phone.

"No," Andy shook his head. "All school activities were cancelled today because of the weather. Even drama club and stuff like that."

"Wow, they're not joking around with this storm," Chantal stated matter-of-factly. "Call Chris and see what's up. I'm going to watch the weather."

"All right," Andy agreed, taking the phone from Chantal. It was strange for him to be calling Chris Dunkin. For the longest time, Chris and Andy had been on complete opposite ends of Montgomery's social realm. For years, Chris had been at the center of the rowdiest clique in their grade, which included Chantal's twin sister Cathy and Cathy's boyfriend Jason. Knowing that Chris and Jason were best friends, Andy had assumed Chris was just as irresponsible and immoral as Jason. For years, it had been impossible to get a splash of Chris without a deluge of Jason.

Chris's other best friend was Jon Anderson. Andy, who liked most people, despised Jon. Jon was Chantal's first love—something Andy had wanted to be—and that bothered him to no end. Jon was well known for his harsh temper, cocky smile, and long list of female admirers.

To Andy's surprise, Chris seemed nothing like his best friends. Andy respected Chris's recent decision to make God the central focus of his life. By attending church weekly with Chantal's family, Andy had witnessed many people find their faith. The change in Chris was, by far, the most dramatic Andy had ever seen. It had challenged Andy to search his own heart much more intricately.

⁂

A few moments later, Jason followed Cathy onto her back porch while looking up at the eerie sky. There was an ominous feeling in the sticky air, and the wind had noticeably picked up since their walk home from school. "We better be quick," Jason said and sat down on the steps that led to the backyard. "Lady better be, too," he added, referring to the Kagellis' golden retriever who had followed them outside.

"You seem extra freaked out about the storm," Cathy commented and sat down beside him.

"The air doesn't feel right," Jason remarked. "It's not going to stop me from smoking this bowl, but otherwise I see no reason to be out here."

While Jason packed his glass bowl tightly with marijuana, he wondered what smoking weed would do to his girlfriend. As far as he knew, she had gone a month without smoking pot or eating edibles, so she had likely lowered her tolerance.

After bringing his lighter to the bowl, he took a large hit and held it in his lungs for ten seconds. After exhaling, he passed the bowl to Cathy. "Don't hit it hard. You still have Klonopin in your system."

Cathy took a small hit and then handed the bowl back to Jason.

"Those clouds look awfully low," Jason observed and pointed off into the horizon, "over in the direction of the high school."

"Well, when I see a wall cloud, I'll run for cover," Cathy remarked offhandedly.

Jason took another long hit off the bowl and then turned his body towards Cathy. "Okay, I need to ask you something," he said hesitantly. "When we were walking home from school, you said you invited Julianna to Alyssa's party because you wanted to get back at Jon and Chantal. Were you serious?"

Cathy looked surprised by his question. "I said that so Alyssa would know my loyalty lies with her," she replied.

"So, you're not holding Jon and Alyssa's breakup against Chantal?"

Cathy shook her head. "No. Chantal had nothing to do with it. Jon mentioned her name just to hurt Alyssa."

"Well, what you said bothered me," Jason admitted. "It was vindictive."

Cathy grabbed the bowl out of Jason's hands.

"And something I never expected from you," he added while eyeing her precariously.

"Julianna and I are friends in school. I don't know if that bothers Alyssa. The only way I felt comfortable asking if I could invite Julianna to the party was by pointing out the trouble it could cause between her and Jon," she explained and passed the bowl back to Jason.

"Alyssa didn't sound like she wants to cause a problem between Jon and Julianna," Jason commented and eyed Cathy expectantly.

"Alyssa's too nice to deliberately cause a problem for anyone. If anything, she'll warn Julianna about Jon's never-ending love for Chantal."

Jason looked up at the sky and wondered if he was just feeling paranoid or if the oncoming clouds were as eerie as they looked. "I think we should go inside," he said and rose slowly from the steps. He emptied his bowl over the side of the railing and then extended his hand to help Cathy to her feet.

"I shouldn't have smoked," she said as she stumbled into the banister.

Jason latched onto Cathy's hand and pulled her toward the house. He felt like he was walking through a wind tunnel. Had the breeze picked up that much? Or was he just really high? After opening the door to the kitchen, he wrapped his arm around Cathy's shoulders and led her upstairs to her bedroom.

"Now I remember why I gave up weed," Cathy mumbled as she flopped down on her bed. Without bothering to get under the covers, she rested her head on a pillow and closed her eyes.

Jason thought back to the time when one hit of weed made Cathy pass out for six hours on his couch because of the anxiety meds in her system. Knowing her parents would be home in less than two hours, he feared that could be the case again. After climbing beside her, he hugged her tightly. She didn't flinch.

Chapter 5

"It's getting pretty bad out," Chantal observed, sitting comfortably with Andy on her bedroom couch. "I'm glad we stayed here. I wouldn't want my little sister home with just Cathy and Jason. They're probably baked out of their minds right now."

"True. Don't worry, though. It's only a thunderstorm," Andy said and kissed her forehead.

"You're probably more scared than I am. Don't forget, I know you very well, Andy Rosetti. Let's stop the movie and put on the weather," Chantal suggested, jumping to her feet. "They said something about a supercell. I don't really know what that is."

"Tal, it's only a *thunderstorm*," Andy stressed, pulling her back down onto the couch. "Don't get up! I'll miss you."

"You'll miss me a lot more if I get sucked up in a tornado!" Chantal exclaimed, returning to her feet. She swiftly made way across her large bedroom to stop the movie. Tuning to the Weather Channel, she froze in her tracks.

⚜

Jason jumped in place as the sound of someone loudly banging on Cathy's bedroom door startled him out of a daze. Feeling confused and disoriented, he sat up in bed and looked down at Cathy, who was still sleeping.

"Cathy! Open up! Now!" Chantal's distressed voice projected from the other side of the door, followed by more knocking.

"Cathy! Jason!" Andy's voice cried out.

Although Jason was still in a bit of a stupor, it was evident to him that Andy and Chantal were panic stricken. As he climbed over Cathy's still body and made way to the door, he struggled to walk straight. He felt like he was moving through some sort of tunnel and realized he was still stoned.

On the other side of the door, someone was frantically turning the locked doorknob. Jason whipped open the door and stared blankly at Chantal and Andy.

"We have to get to the basement!" Chantal exclaimed and ran past Jason into the bedroom. "Cathy, get up!" she cried and tugged on her sister's arm, nearly pulling her off the bed.

"What's going on?" Jason asked, glancing from Chantal to Andy.

"Cathy, get up!" Chantal demanded.

Jason and Andy walked over to the bed, where Cathy was slowly opening her eyes.

"What is it?" she asked in a faint voice.

"Get up! There's a tornado heading toward us. Get up now!" Chantal exclaimed.

Cathy shot her glassy eyes wide open. "What?" she asked, seeming to snap out of a daze.

Chantal grabbed both of Cathy's arms and pulled her upright. "What is wrong with you? Get out of bed!"

Jason was trying to process Chantal's words; however, thinking seemed abnormally difficult. Nevertheless, he knew he needed to get Cathy to the basement. Pushing past Chantal, he pulled

Cathy up from her bed and wrapped his arm tightly around her. "We have to go the cellar," he said to her. "Just lean against me and walk."

Chantal and Andy both gave Jason strange looks before turning out of the room and scurrying down the hallway.

"Hurry!" Chantal yelled before descending the stairs.

Andy stopped short at the top of the stairs. "Do you need help getting her downstairs?" he asked Jason.

"I'm fine," Cathy said and picked up her pace. She stumbled a couple of times into the railing but made it down the first flight of stairs okay.

"Guys, hurry up!" Chantal cried from the first floor.

"Just c'mon!" Andy insisted and tugged on Cathy's arm, pulling her away from Jason and down the second-floor hallway.

As Jason hustled to catch up with them, he acknowledged that Andy was making much better progress with Cathy than he had. Ten seconds later, they were in the kitchen with Chantal and nine-year-old Stephanie. Chantal flung open the basement door and motioned for everyone to run down the steps.

"Get in the middle of the room, away from the windows," she demanded once everyone was safely downstairs.

"What is going on?" Cathy asked as she stood still in the middle of the room.

Chantal glared at her sister. "What is wrong with you? Did you take a sleeping pill or something?" she asked and glanced at Jason.

"She's just tired," Jason responded, although he assumed Chantal could see how glassy and red Cathy's eyes were. He had no idea what time it was or how long they had been in bed. He could not even begin to guess when Cathy's high would wear off. He slumped down against the concrete wall and motioned for Cathy to sit beside him.

"Chantal, why are you making us stay down here?" Cathy whined as she slouched onto the cold cement floor next to Jason.

"There is a tornado warning!" Chantal exclaimed after sitting down beside Andy. "My gosh, Cathy, think for once! Sometimes I wonder if you have any brain cells left at all." She sighed and rested her head on Andy's shoulder. "Are you scared?" she asked as she turned towards her little sister.

Stephanie nodded intently. "Where are Mom and Dad?"

"They're safe at work," Andy replied and embraced Chantal and Stephanie. "Just like you're safe here with us."

"Are you scared?" Stephanie questioned them.

"Not when I'm with you and Andy," Chantal replied.

"Where's Lady?" Stephanie asked. "Lady?" she called out, sitting up straight.

Jason's stomach dropped.

"Oh my gosh!" Chantal cried.

"Where is she?" Andy asked while jumping to his feet.

"I...I...I don't know! Outside?" Chantal stammered.

"I'll be right back," Andy promised and then dashed up the basement stairs.

"Wait!" Chantal exclaimed, but her voice was drowned out by the thunderous boom erupting outside.

Jason widened his eyes. "She's outside," he said as his mind slowly processed what was happening. "She came outside with us earlier, but we didn't bring her back in."

"Lady wasn't outside with us," Cathy stated flatly.

Jason's heart pounded. "We forgot to let her in. We forgot she was out there."

Chapter 6

"Let's go, girl. Come on, Lady!" Andy called, spotting Lady huddled inside her half-collapsed doghouse. Lady arose hesitantly, glancing at her surroundings. "Come on, girl," Andy repeated, making his way closer to the obedient golden retriever. Emerging from her unstable home, Lady leaped toward Andy.

The storm's strength had intensified during the few moments Andy had been outside. His eyes began widening in horror as he watched a funnel cloud begin to form in the eerie, green sky. He wondered if it was only his imagination or if the cloud was truly lowering before his eyes. Sensing the urgency in the air, Lady tugged on Andy's sleeve. Thrusting toward the back porch, Andy and Lady forced their way through the marble-size hail that had begun pelting them from the sky.

A sickening thought crept into Andy's mind as he reached the back porch. He had run out the door without any thought of its lock. Andy began tensely turning the knob—locked. He glanced up at the sky. His imagination had not been running wild; the large funnel cloud was rotating in the distance and advancing toward the ground. Banging on the door with all of his might, Andy screamed at the top of his lungs, "CHANTAL! HELP!"

Lady dashed off. Without hesitation, Andy leaped off the deck and chased after her. He found her scratching and whimpering at the front door. His stomach dropped as a rumble resembling a freight train erupted. Immediately, Andy fell to the ground and began vomiting violently.

⸻✺⸻

"Get down!" Jason yelled across the basement. "Chantal, get down now!"

"I have to find Andy!" Chantal hollered while running toward the stairs.

"Stop!" Stephanie wailed.

The ground began to vibrate, and Chantal fell over hard on her back.

Jason immediately crawled to her side. "Are you okay?" he asked, as loudly as his strained voice could propel.

"Where's Andy?" Chantal sobbed.

The sound of footsteps projected from the stairs. At lightning speed, Lady lunged to the basement floor.

"Where's Andy?!" Chantal screamed.

With adrenaline breaking through his brain fog, Jason darted towards the stairs. He grabbed ahold of the railing as a sound resembling a freight train became apparent. *How is this happening? A tornado in Montgomery?* The door to the basement was ajar, so Jason knew Andy was somewhere in the house. *What is he doing?* Jason's heart pounded as he climbed the stairs, realizing every step he took put himself in greater danger. "Andy?" he yelled, hoping his friend would somehow hear his voice over the twister's rumble.

After getting no response, Jason pushed the door all the way open and prayed the tornado was not about to strike the home. His eyes met Andy's body, lying across the kitchen floor, covered in chunks of plaster from the ceiling. Jason immediately glanced up and widened his eyes. Through the skylight on the cathedral ceiling,

Jason could see that a tree had fallen on the roof, causing the ceiling to start collapsing. The beams going across the room looked sturdy, but if another tree were to fall or if the tornado were to directly strike the house, there was no guarantee any of the heavy wooden beams would stay intact.

"Andy! Andy!" Jason yelled while climbing over his friend to remove the heavy chunks of plaster off his face and chest. He knew it wasn't wise to move an injured person, but leaving Andy in the kitchen posed an even greater threat.

"Chantal!" Jason cried as tears began to fill up his eyes. "Chantal, I need your help! Now!"

Within five seconds, Chantal was on the floor beside Jason, gaping at Andy in horror.

"We need to move him downstairs," Jason directed. "The ceiling might not hold up. Those beams could kill him or us. We have to move."

Chantal stared speechlessly at Andy with wide eyes.

Jason lifted Andy into an upright position and then put his own arms underneath Andy's armpits from behind. As he stood up, he pulled Andy's body up with him. "Chantal," he huffed, "get on the other side of him and put his arm around your shoulders."

"Okay," Chantal replied while breathing heavily.

Together, they slowly made their way down the stairs and positioned Andy up against a wall. Lady immediately began licking Andy's face while Chantal collapsed beside him and sobbed. Jason darted once again up the stairs to close the door. He saw the cordless phone sitting on the nearby table. Dialing 9-1-1 would ensure Andy got the medical attention he needed, but walking across the kitchen would put Jason's own life at risk. Knowing his cell phone had no service in the basement, he decided he had no choice but to grab the phone. As small chunks of plaster fell to the floor in front of him, Jason raced to the phone. After picking it up, he dialed 9-1-1, left it off the hook, and darted back to the basement. When his feet touched the cellar floor, he felt the greatest sense of relief he had ever known. Then he locked his eyes on Andy and felt nothing but despair.

Chapter 7

Cathy sat up against the cellar wall in apparent shock while the medics loaded Andy's body onto a stretcher and took him away by ambulance. She felt as though she had been watching a horror movie. Even though she knew it was real, it did not feel real. Jason, Chantal, and Stephanie were all sobbing, but she could not summon any emotion at all. *This is bad,* she thought. *This is really bad.*

From what she understood, Andy had gone upstairs to let Lady in when he was knocked out by falling plaster. The tornado had not directly struck her house, but the kitchen had been damaged by a falling tree. Whether this had happened five minutes ago or thirty minutes ago, she did not know. *How did we forget to bring Lady downstairs with us?* She could not answer that question because her memory of the afternoon was full of holes.

"Cathy," Jason said as he kneeled down in front of her. "Are you okay?"

She stared at him blankly, wanting to speak but not knowing how.

Jason reached forward to hug her. "Andy will be okay," he said and squeezed her tightly.

She remained completely stoic, unable to respond appropriately to anything taking place.

"Is she in shock?" Chantal asked.

Jason released Cathy from his embrace and eyed her intently. "I think so," he replied. "Cathy, say something."

She blinked and swallowed the large lump that had formed in her throat. "Hi," she said.

"Oh, she'll be fine," Chantal said in an annoyed tone. "I need to get to the hospital. I hope my mom gets home soon."

"The paramedics said the storm's over. It's safe to go upstairs, but it's not safe to be in the kitchen. Take my phone, run upstairs, and bolt out of the kitchen," Jason instructed her while handing her his cell phone. "Call your mom and tell her what happened. She must be on her way home by now. I'm sure she's been trying to reach you."

"Steph, stay down here," Chantal ordered.

Jason glanced at Stephanie. "Andy's going to be okay," he assured her. "We all are."

"What if my mom and dad got caught in the storm?" Stephanie asked as tears seeped from her brown eyes.

"They didn't," Jason replied. "They knew about the storm, so they stayed at work. You'll see."

"Okay," Stephanie said while breathing heavily.

Cathy latched onto Jason's shirt. "How did we forget to bring Lady downstairs?" she asked, finally finding her voice.

Jason's facial expression grew even more grim. "We left her outside by mistake," he replied quietly.

"When? What are you talking about?" Cathy asked.

"Before we went upstairs," Jason replied. "We forgot to bring her inside with us."

Cathy squinted. "I don't remember," she stated honestly. "I don't remember anything."

Jason cocked his head to the side. "I'll walk you through everything later. Let's see what Chantal says. Hopefully we can get a ride to the hospital soon."

"The tornado didn't hit my house, right?" Cathy asked.

Jason shook his head. "Thank God, no, but the paramedics said it tore up the woods nearby."

"We're so lucky," Cathy said and let out a heavy breath. "I don't even remember coming down to the basement."

Jason wrapped Cathy in his arms. "You're just in shock."

Footsteps on the stairs caught Cathy's attention. She turned and saw Chantal and her mother entering the cellar.

"Mom!" Stephanie cried and immediately ran to her side.

Mrs. Kagelli embraced Stephanie tightly and glanced over at Cathy. "Thank God you guys are okay. Dad's just leaving his office now. He's going to meet us at the hospital."

"Are we allowed to see Andy?" Jason asked.

"Mrs. Rosetti called me after the hospital called her. She told me only a few visitors are allowed. I think it would be best if I take Chantal up there now, and you three stay here."

"Okay," Jason agreed. "Just let us know how Andy's doing."

"Of course. Cathy, are you okay?" Mrs. Kagelli asked.

Cathy nodded slowly.

"I think she's in shock," Jason said, "but coming out of it."

"Do you need to go to the hospital?" Mrs. Kagelli asked.

Cathy shook her head. "I'll be okay."

Mrs. Kagelli nodded. "Okay. Let's go upstairs. Then I want you guys to avoid the kitchen. I'll try to bring something home for dinner. I don't know if any restaurants are open. The town looks like a warzone."

"You could drop us off at my house on your way to the hospital," Jason suggested. "Do you know if the tornado hit Hamilton?"

"It went from High Street to downtown," Mrs. Kagelli replied.

"Okay. So, my house should be fine. Cathy and Stephanie can have dinner with my family if that will make things easier on you guys," Jason offered.

Mrs. Kagelli nodded. "That would be great. Call your mom and make sure it's okay. Then we can leave."

Jason extended his hand toward Cathy to lift her up off the floor. "Are you okay with that?" he asked.

Still having a hard time finding any words, Cathy nodded and took her boyfriend's hand. Ten minutes later, she found herself in her mother's car on the way to Jason's, wondering if the gravity of the situation would ever sink in.

Chapter 8

***

"This is all my fault," Chantal moaned, peering at Andy's blank face.

"No, no, Chantal," Mrs. Rosetti comforted her, "Andy should have known better than to leave the basement. He just always tries to make everything perfect."

Chantal, her parents, Andy's parents, and Andy's brother Robby were gathered in Andy's small hospital room. The whole situation seemed surreal to Chantal. When she had seen Andy rush off in search of Lady, she had not imagined it could be the last time she would see him conscious.

Leaning over Andy's hospital bed, Chantal recalled how fervently he had pursued her. She thought of how he had romanced her—first in seventh grade and again after her breakup with Jon. Staring at Andy's blank face, she thought of the somewhat mischievous, curious, twelve-year-old boy she had brought to youth group two years prior. People had told her she was crazy to give Andy a chance or to believe he would ever come to share her faith. Chantal never gave up on him, even while she was dating Jon. After

Jon broke Chantal's heart, Andy had dried her tears and helped her get back on solid ground. He opened his heart up to Chantal and became the supportive boyfriend she had always believed he could be. She did not even want to think about the possibility of losing him.

"He's going to pull through," Mr. Rosetti stated firmly while embracing his wife.

"We need to pray," Chantal's mother said, grabbing ahold of her husband's hand.

Chantal nodded in agreement, taking hold of her mother's other hand. Chantal reached out for Andy's mother, who hesitantly took her hand. Mr. Rosetti and Robby joined the chain, creating a circle around Andy's bed. Chantal's father led them in prayer, asking God to bring Andy out of a coma. He concluded with saying, "Nevertheless, not our will, but let Your will be done. In Jesus' name, Amen."

⋆≫≪⋆

"Coming up next on channel sixty-three's Montgomery News at Ten, is Mayor Angeletti with an emergency speech," an overly enthusiastic reporter announced.

Alyssa sat with her family on their sofa, wondering if the storm was going to ruin the party she had planned. Everyone's eyes were glued to the television. Birdseye-view shots of Montgomery flashed across the screen. Debris and wreckage were scattered everywhere. Sections of roofs floated in the lake, and cars lay upside down in the middle of streets.

Mayor Angeletti's stressed face appeared on the screen. His blonde hair appeared messy and windblown. As he looked into the camera, sweat began dripping down his sun-tanned face.

"Good Evening is not even an appropriate way to start off this speech," he began. "Today's storm has erupted chaos throughout our normally peaceful town. To my knowledge, three homes have been destroyed, and close to fifty have been damaged. It is estimated that the damage caused by today's severe weather outbreak ranges in the millions. Over twenty injuries have been made known to officials. However, no deaths have been reported.

"If you have suffered in any way from this disastrous event, contact me at the Town Hall or at my home: 413-555-0235. The government and insurance agencies will aid you through this crisis. I am scheduling a town-wide meeting tomorrow night at seven in the Town Hall's pressroom, where all these matters will be discussed. I would like for all citizens of Montgomery to come, whether you have been affected or not. We need to work together as a community to rebuild our town.

"All in-town work is cancelled tomorrow, including the pre-school, elementary schools, middle schools, and high school. Any further cancellations will be made known at tomorrow's meeting. Citizens left homeless are invited to stay at the Royal Lake Hotel, compliments of the hotel's owners. Please report any damages that have been made known to you. I believe this is all for now. I need to return home to comfort my own family. By the way, a clear sunny day is in tomorrow's forecast. I do not think I have to advise you to appreciate it. Goodnight, everyone. This speech will re-play on channel sixty-three at eleven o'clock tonight. Thank you sincerely."

Alyssa's eyes were wide when the broadcast concluded. Her party no longer concerned her as she wondered if any of her friends or their homes had been impacted by the supercell. "I'm so glad you made me come home," she admitted to her mother. "I hope everyone we know is okay. I'm going to make some calls."

It was far too late to call Cathy's house, but thankfully Lisa had a cell phone. When Lisa answered, Alyssa felt somewhat relieved. Lisa informed her that her house and her family were fine, but she had not been able to get ahold of Cathy. Before Alyssa could get too worried, Lisa told her that Jason had texted her to make sure she was okay and to let her know that Cathy was safe at his house.

"I don't think anyone we know was impacted by the storm," Lisa said, "so we should all be good to come to your party tomorrow if it's still on."

"Yeah … I mean … if everyone's okay, I'm fine with having it. My parents are still planning to go away, so I don't see any reason to cancel it," Alyssa said.

"Great!" Lisa exclaimed. "So, I'll see you tomorrow. What time should I come over? I can help you get ready."

"Since school is cancelled, my parents, John, and Day are going to leave for New Hampshire around one," Alyssa replied. "Come over any time after that."

"Sounds good!" Lisa cried cheerfully. "I'll probably come with Leslie or Katherine. I'll call before we head over."

When Alyssa hung up the phone, she felt a mixture of excitement about her party and concern for the welfare of her town. She tried to search online for the exact path of the tornado, but it had not yet been reported.

Chapter 9

Cathy sat Stephanie down in the Davids' formal living room and found a Disney movie for her to watch on TV. Their mother was planning to pick them up within a half hour, and Cathy needed some time alone with Jason to talk about all that had transpired. "I'll come check on you in a little bit," Cathy said to her younger sister.

"I didn't know Jason lived in a castle!" Stephanie cried with wide eyes. "How many TVs do they have?"

Cathy smiled. "Too many to count," she replied and turned to leave the room.

Jason was waiting for her in the foyer. "Will she be okay alone for a few minutes?" he asked.

Cathy nodded. "I found her favorite movie on TV. She'll be fine."

"All right, let's go talk in my room," Jason replied and led Cathy upstairs.

After sitting down beside each other on Jason's bed, they both sat in silence for a few seconds. Cathy didn't know where to begin. Her head was full of disorderly thoughts.

Jason let out a heavy breath. "I can't believe he hasn't woken up yet. It's been six hours. That's not good."

"If we were the ones who left Lady outside, then why did Andy go get her?" Cathy asked. "Why didn't one of us go?"

Jason hung his head. "It should have been me. I was too stoned to react before Andy bolted up the stairs. If anything happens to him, I don't think I'll be able to live with myself. I knew the sky looked bad. We never should have smoked with a storm like that on its way."

"Are you sure we let Lady out?" Cathy questioned him.

"Positive."

"Why can't I remember anything?" Cathy asked with frustration.

Jason took a deep breath. "You smoked on Klonopin," he replied matter-of-factly. "Honestly, you're lucky Andy and I were able to get you to the basement."

Cathy swallowed the lump that had formed in her throat. "None of this seems real," she admitted. "I mean, when was the last time a tornado hit Massachusetts?"

"We knew it was coming. There's no excuse for what we did."

Cathy widened her eyes. "Why do you sound so condemned?"

"Because Andy's in the hospital, and it's all my fault," Jason replied. "He's a good person. He deserves none of this."

"It's not your fault he ran out of the basement!" Cathy protested. "That was his choice."

"To save your dog!" Jason cried. "Anyone sober enough to think would have done the same thing. We were useless because we were stoned."

"So, you think it's my fault, too?" Cathy asked.

"It's more my fault than yours," Jason said and let out a heavy breath. "It was my weed. I should have known better than to let you smoke. I knew you were only doing it to appease me."

"I remember sitting on the back deck and then nothing else until the paramedics came into the basement."

"Well, I remember everything. Andy looked dead when I found him. I'll never get that image out of my mind."

"But you brought him downstairs. You saved him from getting hit by more of the ceiling. That counts for something."

Jason let out a short laugh. "No. It counts for nothing. He wouldn't have been up there if it wasn't for our mistake. If anything happens to him, it's on us."

Cathy lowered her eyebrows and glared at Jason. "How can you say that?"

Jason widened his eyes. "How can you not?"

Cathy shrugged. "Whether we let Lady out or Chantal let her out, the decision to leave the basement was Andy's."

"I hate what benzos do to you," Jason stated sadly and shook his head.

"I'm sure the Klonopin I took earlier has worn off by now."

Jason looked up at the ceiling and let out a heavy breath. "You didn't even cry."

"I'm upset. I was just in shock. I couldn't respond."

"I know, but you're not in shock now, and you're still not crying."

"Well, I'm hoping my mom will arrive with good news," Cathy retorted.

"There's not going to be any good news," Jason said with his voice cracking. "He would have already woken up."

"I'm worried about Andy," Cathy insisted. "I'm worried about Chantal and Lisa, too. I'm sure they're both devastated."

"Alyssa should cancel her party," Jason stated flatly. "If Andy is still in the hospital tomorrow, I won't feel right celebrating anything."

Cathy shrugged. "Maybe a party is what people need to get their minds off the storm? Maybe being together would be good for everyone? A party could be a nice distraction."

Jason lowered his eyebrows and glared at her. "What is wrong with you?" he questioned her in a tone filled with disgust. "Our friend is probably in a coma."

"We don't know that."

"Cathy, c'mon. I thought he was dead."

"Well, he's not."

Jason scowled. "The only reason I would go to Alyssa's tomorrow would be to tell people about Andy."

"Don't do that!" Cathy exclaimed. "His family might not want everyone knowing. It's their place to tell people—not ours—and that news would kill the vibe of the party."

Jason widened his eyes. "You need to go downstairs and wait for your mom with Stephanie. I can't have this conversation. Our friend could be on his deathbed, and you're worried about killing the vibe of a $%&@ Halloween party?!"

Cathy stared at Jason blankly. He sure sounded angry.

"Just get out," he stated downheartedly and pointed toward the door. "I'm going to bed. Don't call me unless you have news about Andy."

"Okay," Cathy said flatly and stood up from the bed. "I think sleep's a good idea. You're being a bit dramatic."

Jason rolled his eyes and fell back onto his bed.

Without saying another word, Cathy walked out the door, wondering when what happened to Andy would faze her.

Chapter 10

One Day Later

"Peppermint schnapps?" Cathy asked, waving the pint before Julianna Camen's innocent blue eyes.

Julianna shrugged. "Um, okay."

Cathy threw the glass bottle onto her bed and began searching through her bureau drawer.

"Do you do this before every party?" Julianna asked while examining the bottle.

"It depends on who I'm with," Cathy replied.

"Well, who?" Julianna questioned her.

Cathy sighed and turned to Julianna. Two souvenir shot glasses were in her hands. Carefully stepping over her many belongings on the hardwood floor, she made way to her bed. "Are you trying to figure out who does all this stuff or something?" she asked as she sat down beside Julianna.

"Well, no. I don't know," Julianna stammered.

"Hmm, let me think," Cathy said slowly while opening the bottle. A fresh peppermint scent filled the air. "Alyssa and Lisa are my best friends, so I'm usually with one of them or Jason. Alyssa doesn't like smoking weed, but she'll drink with me. Jay's pretty much the opposite. He's a much bigger fan of narcotics than alcohol. We usually just take whatever his brother Luke gives us. That always makes for an interesting night! I think Lisa's the worst of all. She gets high every day."

"Lisa who?"

"Ankerman," Cathy clarified as she poured a shot of alcohol into Julianna's glass. "But she does not drink at all—not a drop. Ever since her dad died in that accident, she's been completely afraid of alcohol."

Julianna's jaw dropped. "Our class rep is a pothead?"

"Julianna, I hate to break your naïve little heart, but a lot of people seem different than they really are. It's called a front."

"That is so surprising."

"You just never know what people do behind closed doors. Everyone thinks Lisa, Andy, and all their preppy friends are angels, but you would be surprised. I do know for a fact that my sister is against drugs. Andy keeps a *lot* of things from her," Cathy emphasized, rolling her eyes. "She wouldn't date him if she knew the things I know about him. I learned a while ago not to interfere with her relationships."

Julianna smiled. "Chantal's awesome. You have to admit that. I know you guys are not friends, but you're lucky to have her for a sister. She's so nice to everybody."

Cathy smiled awkwardly before taking her shot. When she turned back to Julianna, her eyes watered. "Aren't you going to drink that?" she asked, pointing to the shot glass in Julianna's hand. Without waiting for an answer, she poured herself a second shot. "Or am I going to drink by myself?" She was determined to forget about her fight with Jason, Andy's accident, and the storm so she could have a fun night. Luckily, Julianna didn't know about Andy's injury, so Cathy didn't have to talk about it.

Julianna was staring at Cathy nervously. "No," she replied a few seconds later before slowly tipping back her shot.

Cathy watched her with amusement. "Well?"

"This tastes like mouthwash!" Julianna cried as she wiped her lips.

"It really does," Cathy laughed and refilled Julianna's glass.

Jon Anderson sighed, staring blankly at the movie flashing before his pain-filled eyes. Seeing a movie with two happy couples, after just breaking up with Julianna, was far from enjoyable. At least Marielle and Chris were watching the movie. Courtney and Bryan, on the other hand, seemed a bit preoccupied with each other.

What had Jon seen in Julianna besides insecurity? He had wanted to rescue her from herself. He had tried to share his faith with her, but she had remained pessimistic. After only a few weeks of dating her, Jon had grown annoyed with Julianna's superficial words and values. He had realized that she would never replace Chantal, and that even though he wanted to help her, their relationship would not last long.

Despite all the encouragement Jon had given Julianna, she had ditched him for his ex-girlfriend's party. Jon knew Julianna's insecurities were going to get her in way over her head. He had once been in her position. He didn't want Julianna to make the mistake he had. When he caved to temptation in seventh grade, he turned his back on his faith and lost sight of everything he'd grown up valuing. Where did it get him? He lost the only girl he had ever loved and the knowledge of his own identity.

When Julianna accepted Cathy's party invitation, Jon realized his rescue mission had failed. Julianna was in for a bumpy ride down a long road in search of fulfillment. Unfortunately for her, nothing remotely near that road had the ability to fulfill.

Jason Davids glanced at his bedroom clock. Seven nineteen. Twenty-four hours had passed since one of the darkest moments of his life. He sighed and fell back on his unmade bed. He curled into the fetal position and tried with all of his might to will the horrifying image out of his mind.

He had not slept a wink in thirty-seven hours. He glanced at his clock again: seven twenty. *You can do this Jason*, he said to himself. *Just get up and go. Go tell them the truth. Tell everyone at Alyssa's party that you found Andy's body. Tell them that he looked dead. Tell them about the horror in Chantal's eyes when she came rushing up the stairs. Make sure you tell them that it is all your fault.*

"Jay-Dawg, you ready?" Luke called, tapping on Jason's bedroom door. "We have to pick up Laurelle and Missy on the way," he added, whipping open the door.

Jason sat up in his bed and rested his head in his hands.

Luke's face fell as he glanced at his younger brother.

"Yeah," Jason sighed, "I'm good."

"You're going to this party in a t-shirt and sweatpants?" Luke questioned him, taking a seat at Jason's desk and staring at him with amusement.

"Oh," Jason said, as if the thought of getting dressed had not occurred to him. "No, I guess I'm not."

"What drug are you on right now?" Luke laughed.

"None," Jason stated flatly, staring blankly at his feet.

"Then what the hell is wrong with you?" Luke asked.

Jason shrugged.

"All right, well get dressed and come downstairs when you're ready," Luke said, eyeing Jason with concern.

Jason nodded slightly.

"Did you sleep last night?" Luke pressed.

"No."

"You and Cathy all right?" Luke asked, holding his stare on Jason.

Jason shrugged.

"Well, freshen up. I'll see you in a few," Luke stated, tossing something at Jason as he exited the room.

Lifelessly, Jason glanced at the minuscule bag of white powder that had landed beside him on his bed. If he had the energy, his eyes would have protruded from his face in horror. "You have got to be kidding me, Luke," he heaved, shaking his head in dismay.

He flung the bag onto his floor, fell back on his bed, and closed his eyes. *You can do this, Jason. Just get dressed and get out the door, right now. Bring out the charm and the plastic smile. Forget what Cathy said. Just get up and face the facts. You've a made a mess of a good person's life. You have to tell them the truth. It doesn't matter what Cathy wants. Andy is all that matters now.*

Chapter 11

Mrs. Kagelli drove Julianna and Cathy to Alyssa's around eight o'clock. She was so concerned about Andy that she remained oblivious to the girls' intoxication. As Julianna and Cathy stumbled into Alyssa's two-story foyer, heads turned from all directions.

"You came!" Alyssa greeted them, throwing her slender arms around Julianna. "I'm so glad. You look great!"

"You, too," Julianna responded slowly, squinting her glossy eyes. "Alyssa?"

"Yeah, it's me!" Alyssa cried. "I guess Cathy got you pretty drunk, huh? Well, have fun!" she exclaimed before bouncing off to greet other guests.

Julianna separated from Cathy and began searching through the Kelly's immaculate mansion. She wasn't sure whom she was in search of, but she felt it was urgent to find them.

"Julianna?" Leslie Lucus questioned her as the two girls collided in the dining room.

"Huh?" Julianna replied, turning to face Leslie.

"What's wrong with you?" Leslie asked wide-eyed. "You look like you're going to fall over."

"Did you just get here?" Julianna asked, steadying herself against the mahogany table.

Leslie shook her head. "No, Lisa and I were the first ones here. Kat's on her way."

"You seem sober."

"I am!" Leslie exclaimed. "Just because you go to a party doesn't mean you have to drink. I'm leaving at eleven with Lisa and Kat."

"Oh," Julianna replied, losing interest in the conversation. Before tonight, she would have been hanging on Leslie's every word. Leslie was one of the most popular girls in school, but suddenly popularity didn't matter to Julianna.

"Hi, guys!" a perky voice cried out. Julianna tried to focus on the girl who was approaching them.

"Hi, Kat!" Leslie exclaimed while giving her friend a hug. "You know Julianna, right?"

Katherine Rossi studied Julianna. "I know *of* Julianna, but I never expected to see her *here*."

"I came here with Cathy," Julianna stated defensively.

"I think you better go lie down," Katherine suggested. "You look sort of sick."

"Well, she is sort of drunk," Leslie explained.

"I can tell," Katherine replied. "You're friends with Cathy?"

Julianna shrugged. "I guess."

"Do you know Bobby Ryan?"

"Math class, yup!" Julianna exclaimed.

"Was he over Cathy's, too?"

"Ladies!" Jason yelled, interrupting Katherine's quiz as he walked up to the girls. He threw his arms around Leslie and Julianna without hesitation.

"Hi, Jay," Leslie greeted him casually.

"What's wrong?" Jason asked, turning toward Julianna. "I don't get a 'hello' from you?"

"Stop yelling!" Julianna demanded. "You're hurting my head."

"Julianna, why don't you go lie down?" Katherine urged her.

"You know, you're actually kind of hot!" Jason laughed.

"Why are you being nice? You're not nice," Julianna shot back, ignoring Katherine's suggestion as she glared at Jason.

"Aww, I just tease you in school because you're so quiet. I just try to get a rise out of you. Don't even listen to me," Jason replied, sounding somewhat remorseful. "I have nothing against you."

"Really?" Julianna asked, stunned that he was being polite. Jason was the most intimidating guy in their grade.

"Yeah," Jason nodded, smiling slightly, "but for your best interest, don't tell my girlfriend I said that."

"Where *is* Cathy?" Julianna asked.

"I don't know. I haven't seen her," Jason replied distractedly. "Guys, I kind of had a reason for coming over here. Sorry to interrupt, but … Leslie, you came with Lisa?"

Leslie nodded. "Yeah, but I can't find her."

"Can I talk to you for a minute?" Jason asked in a sobering tone.

Leslie lowered her eyebrows and eyed Jason uncomfortably. "Um, okay. What's up?" she asked nervously.

Immediately, Jason's disposition became unnervingly somber. He let out a heavy breath and dropped his eyes to the floor.

"Um, I'm going to leave you guys alone ... yeah ... I think I'll go sit down ... somewhere," Katherine stammered while backing away from Jason.

"I'll go find Cathy," Julianna said, also quickly backing away from Jason. Even though she was drunk and feeling rather carefree, she still found him intimidating.

⁂

This movie is way too long! Jon's mind was enraged. He needed to warn Julianna about his old friends. She was innocent, naïve, and weak. Julianna was a follower with absolutely no foundation to stand on. "Chris?" he called, turning to face his best friend.

"Yeah?" Chris responded, without turning his head away from the movie screen.

"We have to go to that party," Jon demanded. "I have to get Julianna out of there."

"Now?" Chris questioned Jon, turning to face him. "The movie's almost over. Can't we wait?"

"What's going on?" Bryan asked from the other side of Jon.

"I want to go to Alyssa's and talk to Julie," Jon explained. "She's definitely in trouble."

"Court, are you up for a party?" Bryan questioned her, turning back to his girlfriend.

"Alyssa's? Are you serious, Bryan?!" Courtney rebuked him.

"Who's going to a party?" Marielle asked, snuggling against Chris's muscular arm.

"I want to see Julie," Jon repeated loudly. "She's going to get in way over her head."

"Jon, she wanted to go," Courtney stated with aggravation. "She ditched us for them. Who needs a friend like that?"

"Yeah but, Court," Marielle interrupted her, "it was a different story when you ditched us for them, right?"

Courtney sighed and fell silent.

"Well, I'm up for the party," Bryan stated.

"I never cancelled plans with you or Julianna!" Courtney cried while leaning across Bryan and Jon so Marielle could hear her. "Plus, I invited you to sit with me at lunch!"

"You invited me and made Julie cry," Marielle retorted. "You weren't a good friend to her when *you* hung out with Cathy and Alyssa."

"I've seen this movie already," Chris said, suddenly jumping up from his seat. "I guess I'm up for making an appearance."

"So, you guys will come?" Jon asked.

"Yeah, let's jet," Courtney agreed sadly, standing up from her seat.

"Don't be sad, Court," Bryan soothed, brushing a piece of her silky black hair from her face.

"Besides," Chris said as he draped his arm around Marielle's shoulders, "everyone will be so blazed they won't even remember they're your enemies. They're not going to bother you, Court."

Chapter 12

"That's her house," Jon said a half hour later, pointing to a charming Victorian mansion. His stomach suddenly dropped. Alyssa had been his best friend for nearly a decade before they dated. He had broken up with her in a fit of rage, humiliating both Alyssa and himself in front of all their friends. They had not spoken since the incident. He regretted hurting her and would not blame her if she refused to let him inside her house.

"I've never been to a party like this before," Marielle admitted. "What if I go home smelling like beer and smoke?"

"You're sleeping over my house," Courtney reminded her. "My parents won't even notice. My sister and her friends used to get high—right in Day's bedroom—and my parents never suspected a thing! My dad can run a town a lot better than a household."

"Day?!" Marielle exclaimed in awe.

Courtney nodded. "Oh yeah. Alyssa's brother even broke up with her for a while because she got so out of control. I don't really know the specifics, but she got into some drugs."

"Really?" Marielle asked.

"Yeah. She ended up missing John a lot more than she thought she would. Somehow, he convinced her to go to church with him. The more she went, the more she realized drugs were messing up her life. I love my sister now that she's sober. I'm excited about her and John's engagement."

"Even though marriage will link Alyssa to your family?" Marielle asked facetiously.

Courtney rolled her eyes.

"Chris, are you sure you want to go inside? You don't think it will bother you to be around everyone and everything?" Bryan asked.

"I'm not worried about it," Chris replied.

"Chris, please don't leave my side," Marielle said nervously.

"I won't," Chris promised and kissed the top of Marielle's head. "I know you'll feel out of place, Mar, but none of these people have a problem with you. They'll just ignore you."

"Good," Marielle said and entered the Kellys' elegant foyer.

"Let's check the kitchen," Jon hollered over the hip-hop blaring from the surround sound.

After entering the kitchen, they all did a double take.

"Is that her over there with Cathy?" Marielle asked, gesturing toward a skimpily dressed blonde.

As Jon laid his brown eyes on Julianna, he felt fury rise up inside of him. "What the … what did they do to her?" he cried, pushing through the crowded kitchen. "Julianna!"

"Jon?" Julianna called, turning around to face him. "Hi!" she exclaimed brightly.

"You look like a slut! What has gotten into you?" he yelled.

Julianna shrugged carelessly. "Just some alcohol. Do you want some?" she offered, bringing her daiquiri to Jon's lips.

"Don't do this," Jon said, pushing the drink away from his face. "Don't become one of her clones," he pleaded, glaring at Cathy.

Julianna stared at Jon for a hard second. "You know, your good-guy act is getting really old. You just want to sleep with me, just like everyone else you ever dated. It's no secret. You're a player, just like the rest of your friends," Julianna retorted and pushed past him.

Jon stood in silence, sure that the color had completely drained from his face. He should have expected slander, knowing that Julianna had spent the last six hours with Cathy. The fact that he had never made a move on Julianna was suddenly irrelevant to her. Julianna was naïve enough to believe every smooth word that flowed from Cathy's mouth. After dating both Chantal and Alyssa, Jon had become very familiar with Cathy's manipulative tactics. Her seemingly nonchalant comments, said with a glistening smile, planted seeds deeply in people's minds. She managed to wrap everyone in her social realm tightly around her finger, day after day. Jon could not believe how blind Jason was to it. Over the course of two years, Cathy had completely brainwashed him. It was so sick, twisted, and satanic that Jon could barely stomach spending time with Jason anymore.

Suddenly, the party around Jon seemed to freeze. The scene seemed all too familiar to him. Hadn't the same exact thing happened to him two months ago at Jason's party? He had lost Alyssa to the partying scene. All of a sudden, he understood how Chantal had felt two years prior; he had done the exact same thing to her. Jon hung his head and sighed.

***

It was during seventh grade. Jon and Chantal were walking down his street on their way to Chris's house. Chris's parents had gone away, leaving his cousin Taylor in charge. Taylor had found it absolutely necessary to throw a large soiree in celebration of Mr. and Mrs. Dunkin's absence.

"Jon, don't you worry about Chris at all?" Chantal asked, walking hand in hand with her boyfriend.

Jon shrugged. "He's just having a good time."

49

"Yeah, but he's your best friend. You wouldn't want to see him hurt himself," Chantal replied in a concerned tone. "I wouldn't want to see Alyssa start drinking all the time or start smoking. We're only thirteen. I know it feels like we're old, but at this age we can do a lot of damage to our future."

"Chantal, Chris is fine. He only drinks when his cousins are around, and everyone smokes," Jon said defensively.

"What are you talking about, 'everyone smokes'?" Chantal asked, pulling her hand out of Jon's grip. "We don't."

"I know that," Jon sang, grabbing Chantal's hand. "I just mean it's not a big deal. It's just something people try at our age. It's not like he's smoking pot or anything."

"Yet," Chantal sighed, turning away from her boyfriend.

"Tal, are you mad at me or something?" Jon asked, stopping in the middle of the street and swinging Chantal around to face him.

"No, I just thought you were against all this stuff. Now you're taking me to some party, and you seem fine with it all," Chantal stated. "It just worries me that you don't see Chris has a problem. It makes me think you could be next."

Jon's jaw dropped. "How could you say that? You know me better than that. I'm not going to rain on Chris's parade, but that doesn't mean I'm going to join the marching band."

Chantal laughed, "You wouldn't look so hot wearing a beret."

Jon smiled. "Please. I could rock that look," he joked and squeezed her hand as they continued walking toward Chris's house.

***

Standing in Alyssa's kitchen two years later, Jon felt like the floor had been ripped out from under him. Chantal had been right all along; Chris did have a problem, and Jon would have been next if he hadn't lost Chantal. Jon recalled how he had ended up getting drunk for the first time at that party, and how upset Chantal had been when she found out. A month later, he had caved into his friends' pressure and gotten high for the first time. Right before Chantal's eyes, Jon had thrown away their relationship for temporary pleasure. It was one of the biggest mistakes of his life.

Julianna was making the same mistake he and Alyssa had. Jon knew Julianna did not care about him as much as he cared for Chantal, but he hoped that losing their relationship might enlighten her somehow. Shortly after Chantal broke up with Jon, he had decided she was justified in doing so. He had stopped being involved in their church, started partying with his friends, and pushed all his morals aside. He had later realized if he wanted a second chance with Chantal, he could not follow his friends' path.

"Jon Anderson?" a sober female voice called out from behind him. "What are *you* doing here?"

"Katherine?" Jon asked, turning to face the girl as he escaped from his daze.

"Hi!" Katherine exclaimed while embracing Jon in her arms. "Why are you here?"

Jon shrugged and took one last look at Julianna over Katherine's shoulder. "I don't even know. Where's Bobby?"

Katherine's face fell. "We broke up yesterday. Actually, he dumped me."

"He dumped you?!" Jon exclaimed in disbelief. "Why?"

Katherine shrugged. "He's been so busy with football lately that he really hasn't had any time to spend with me. I mentioned to him last week that I was unhappy. Then yesterday, we were on the phone, and he told me he didn't want to go out anymore. I was shocked. I never thought we'd break up."

"Well, he must be crazy to break up with you," Jon said. Katherine was adorable. She was in all advanced classes, involved in student council, and on the Varsity cheerleading squad. People often mistook her for a snob, but Jon knew she was just shy. They had known each other since elementary school, but once Jon and his friends started partying, Katherine had shied away from them.

Katherine blushed slightly. "I talked to a very drunk Julianna earlier. She told me you two broke up."

Jon sighed. "Yeah. She's different than I thought she was. She made a big mistake by coming here and hanging out with Cathy."

"I didn't want to come either," Katherine admitted and put her head down. "Leslie convinced me it would cheer me up, so I came."

"Well, has it worked?" Jon asked distractedly as he watched Julianna leave the room with Alyssa.

"Not until now," Katherine replied and smiled at Jon.

Jon's thoughts of Julianna were stolen away by Katherine's words. "Why now?" he laughed in disbelief that she would ever flirt with him.

Katherine shrugged. "It's nice to see you."

Jon looked at Katherine strangely as a hesitant smile spread across his lips. "It's always nice to see you," he replied.

"Well, I'm going to look for Lisa and Leslie, but I'll see you around," Katherine said and brushed past Jon.

"Bye," he called, turning around to watch her petite figure move through the party.

"Wow, guy," Chris said, patting Jon on the shoulder as he appeared beside him. "Was that just Katherine Rossi talking to you?"

Jon smiled. "Yeah, she and Bobby broke up."

"What?" Chris asked, sounding shocked. "Why did she breakup with him? Bobby must be a wreck."

Jon shook his head. "No, guy. He broke up with her."

Chris eyed Jon strangely. "That can't be right. He told me at football practice on Wednesday that he wasn't going to play next season because of her."

"She didn't want him to play, and she's a Varsity cheerleader?" Jon asked, finding the whole situation somewhat jilted.

Chris shrugged. "I don't know, dude. That doesn't make much sense. Then again, what do we know about their drama circle?"

Chapter 13

Katherine grew more and more concerned as she continued moving through Alyssa's large home. Where were Lisa and Leslie? After her conversation with Jon, Katherine had begun searching diligently for her two best friends. It was bad enough that Bobby had not shown up; now it seemed as though she was completely friendless at an event she had not wanted to attend in the first place.

"Katherine, is everything okay?" Chris asked after the third time she passed by him in the living room.

"I can't find my friends," Katherine replied, finding it odd that Chris had spoken to her. She knew that Chris and Bobby were football buddies and thought it could be beneficial to speak with him. However, during the last twenty minutes of searching for Lisa and Leslie, Katherine's thoughts of Bobby had greatly diminished.

"Who, Lis and Lee?" Chris questioned her, looking concerned as he stood up from his chair.

"Yeah," Katherine replied, wondering why he would care.

"We can help you look," Chris offered, placing his arm around Marielle's shoulders. "Have you checked upstairs?"

"Um, no. I felt funny going up there," Katherine admitted. "Alyssa isn't a close friend of mine."

Chris laughed. "Come on, let's go up there. Alyssa's too drunk to care at this point."

"Okay," Katherine agreed, following Chris and Marielle into the foyer. She had no idea why Chris was being nice to her but gladly accepted his kindness without explanation. As they made their way up the L-shaped staircase, the noise from the party began to fade away.

"Let's check Alyssa's room," Chris said once he reached the second-floor hallway.

Katherine and Marielle trailed behind him, turning right onto an adjoining hall. Chris paused at a door halfway down the hallway and knocked on it loudly. Jason whipped Alyssa's bedroom door open, revealing Cathy, Lisa, and Leslie inside. Relief rushed over Katherine's face as she spotted her two best friends. It took a moment for her to realize both of them were teary-eyed. Rushing into the room, Katherine took a seat between Lisa and Leslie on Alyssa's bed.

"All right, you found them, Katherine. I'll see you later," Chris said while taking Marielle's hand. "Jay," he nodded in greeting before walking away.

"I should have called and told you before the party. I just wasn't thinking straight," Cathy said as she took a seat beside Lisa.

"What's going on?" Katherine asked slowly, startled by the tears that had begun pouring from Lisa's green eyes.

Lisa looked up at Katherine, unable to speak. She shook her head and dropped it back down.

"Will somebody please tell me what's wrong?" Katherine pleaded, glancing up at Jason. She observed the unfamiliar, concerned look on his face.

Jason let out a heavy breath. "Andy's in the hospital," he said. "He got hurt yesterday during the storm, and uh, they don't know if he's going to make it."

Chapter 14

A half-hour later, Jason trucked heavily down the main staircase to Alyssa's foyer. Moving quickly through the room and tossing anyone who got in his way to the side, Jason breezed into the kitchen. His watery eyes darted around the room rapidly. He spotted Bryan hugging Courtney by the sink, Jon standing nearby with a girl he had never seen before, and Alyssa sitting on the counter with Julianna. He shot his eyes once more around the crowded kitchen and then walked back into the foyer.

After seeing who had shown up at the party, Jason realized no one knew about Andy's accident. When Jason ran into Lisa that night, he had immediately pulled her aside. Lisa was Andy's best friend—someone Jason thought would have heard the news. Even she had been left in the dark. When Cathy found Jason hugging Lisa and Leslie in Alyssa's room, she had shot him an icy glare. Jason didn't care if she was angry with him; she was acting insane.

Hustling into the living room, Jason found Chris sitting with Marielle on the piano bench. He startled both of them when he rushed to their sides. "Dude, we need to talk," Jason stated, eyeing his ex-best friend sternly.

"Okay, so talk," Chris shrugged, pasting his light blue eyes on Jason.

"No, it's not like that," Jason said, shaking his head. "We can't talk here. This is serious, dude. I'm not joking."

Marielle and Chris look stunned when Jason's eyes began filling with tears. Chris nodded and stood up from the bench. A look of deep concern washed over his face. "Are you okay staying here for a while, Marielle?" he asked, glancing from Jason to his girlfriend.

"I'll go find Courtney. I'm fine," she nodded intently.

"Are you sure? I told you I wouldn't leave you, and I don't want you to feel weird," Chris said.

"I'm sure," Marielle stated, warily eyeing Jason. She shot a worried glance in Chris's direction before scurrying out of the living room.

"Let's go outside," Jason said, gesturing toward the foyer. Silently, Chris followed Jason through Alyssa's house and onto the back porch. Jason ignored the strange looks sent in their direction. Chris had been Jason's best friend since kindergarten, so what the heck was everyone's problem?

Following Jason out onto Alyssa's back porch sent flashbacks through Chris's mind. He couldn't count on two hands the number of times he had gone out there to get high. Nevertheless, he could tell from the look on Jason's face that this rendezvous had nothing to do with drugs.

Chris took a seat on top of the picnic table and eyed Jason curiously. Jason began pacing back and forth and eventually sat down in a nearby patio chair.

"Are you in trouble or something?" Chris asked, breaking the awkward silence.

"Nah, dude," Jason said and shook his head. "I wish it was something stupid like that."

Chris swallowed deeply.

"There was an accident yesterday at Cathy's," Jason began slowly, looking at the ground while he spoke, "during the storm.

Andy had gone to let Lady in because Cathy forgot to before we went down to the basement. It should have been me, guy. You know, it was my girlfriend who let the dog out. I knew that, and I should have gone. I just sat there like a wuss and did nothing."

"What happened to Andy?" Chris interrupted him.

Jason looked up at Chris, swallowed deeply, and hung his head. "The rumble from the nearby tornado was so great that ... that ... I guess it caused some things to start collapsing inside the house," Jason said slowly. He became more choked up with every syllable. "He made it as far as the basement door. He got Lady to safety. But the ceiling ... in the kitchen ... it ... it didn't hold up."

"What?!" Chris exclaimed. "Is Andy okay? I mean, he's still alive, right?"

Jason nodded. "He's in intensive care at the hospital. He's been in a coma since the storm." As he looked up at Chris, tears plunged from his eyes. "It should have been me. Not Andy. Andy's too good of a person to have something like this happen to him. I'm an idiot. What good do I bring to this world?"

Chris stared at Jason in awe. "Do they think he's going to be okay?"

Jason shook his head and brought his hands to his forehead. "They don't know if he's going to wake up. I guess it's in God's hands now."

Chris breathed deeply and placed his face inside his hands while trying to gather his thoughts. "Why doesn't anyone know about this?" he asked.

"I don't think Chantal or her parents have talked to anyone. They're really upset right now. I don't know anything about Andy's family. I assumed they told Lisa, but she had no idea until I told her upstairs. I'm guessing Bobby Ryan knows because he didn't show up tonight. I don't know why Cathy doesn't want people to know. I couldn't not tell you guys about something I'm responsible for."

"Jay, listen to me. Everything happens for a reason, okay?" Chris stated sternly. "You can't sit there and say it should have been you because if God wanted it to be you, then it would have been. Do you actually think we have that much control over our lives? There is a reason why this happened, and one day we'll understand it. Right now, we just have to pray that God spares Andy's life. Like you said, it's in His hands now."

"It's just a figure of speech," Jason replied, unable to peel his eyes off the ground. "I wasn't trying to take the blame off myself or anything. I can't just sit there like Cathy and blame someone else for what I did. She's been saying Chantal forgot to let the dog in. And you know what? Chantal *actually* believes she forgot to let Lady in. But actually, Chantal didn't even know Lady was outside. It's so messed up."

"Hey, that's what you get for dating the evil twin," Chris said with a small laugh.

Jason looked up at Chris and rolled his eyes. "Yeah, I know," he said and wiped his moist cheek with the sleeve of his dress shirt.

"So, is Chantal a big mess?" Chris asked.

"Yeah, she is," Jason replied, rubbing his forehead. "I feel so bad for her. I just want to punch Cathy for lying to her. You should have seen her face when we found Andy. I tried to tell her the truth, but she was already convinced she could have done something."

"Well, I'm trying to tell you the truth right now," Chris interrupted. "You couldn't have done anything to prevent this. It's God's will."

Jason laughed. "You know, it's really funny to hear you talk like this."

"I'm sure it is, but it's the truth."

"I think I actually like talking to you more now than I did before. At least you're not trying to tell me there are purple robots outside my window."

Chris felt his face turn bright red. "Um, yeah. At least not that."

"Mescaline," Jason laughed.

Chris shook his head and tried to stop a smile from spreading across his lips. He knew he shouldn't laugh at a time like this, but he couldn't believe how dense he had once been. Why had seeing false mirages been more appealing to him than seeking the truth?

Chapter 15

Chris and Jason continued to converse outside until Bryan stepped onto the porch. "Is everything all right out here?" he asked, dumbfounded that Chris and Jason were conversing.

"Yeah," Chris replied. "It's cool."

Bryan glanced strangely at Chris and then shrugged. "Well, my dad's going to be here in ten minutes. If you want a ride home, be ready."

"Well, I think I'm about ready to go find Marielle," Chris said, standing up from the picnic table. "Jay—what we talked about—let's get to work on it. All right?"

Jason nodded and rose from his chair. "First thing tomorrow, bro," he said and cupped hands with Chris.

Bryan again glanced strangely from Chris to Jason. He noticed that it looked like Jason had been crying but decided he was probably just high. Although Jason had been Bryan's close friend for years, he preferred that Chris keep his distance from him. Chris was almost two months sober, and Bryan knew he could easily relapse. Ironically, Chris had been the one to introduce Jason to the worst vices in his life. Now, Jason posed the threat of corruption to Chris's sobriety, and Chris was becoming a role model.

When Bryan first began dating Courtney in seventh grade, he lost himself in her. He pulled away from his friends and spent every free second he had with her. Falling quickly in love with Courtney had made it easy for Bryan to forget about alcohol, parties, and drugs. He had become friends with Jason, Chris, and Jon long before any of those things mattered. When they had become friends, T-ball and who owned the better Power Wheels had been topics of choice.

Years later, the divide between Chris and Jason posed a great threat to their foursome. Bryan had begun to wonder if he and his best friends would end up going separate ways. It was common for friends to do so after entering high school. People would become friends with older crowds or get involved with sports. Others would change so much that ghosts of their prior selves would not even exist. Bryan had heard stories of such things happening, but he'd always thought his friends would be different. He did not want to sacrifice the bonds of friendship for the sake of growing up.

Courtney and Marielle were waiting by the kitchen table when Bryan, Chris, and Jason entered the kitchen. The two girls appeared to be having a deep conversation. They kept glancing from one another to Julianna, who was standing nearby with Alyssa. Bryan sighed, wondering how it was possible to have so much drama under one roof.

"So, guys, there's something I have to tell you as soon as I get the chance," Chris said as he and Bryan met up with the girls. "Here isn't a good place."

"What happened, Chris? Is everything all right with Jason?" Marielle asked with concern.

Chris nodded. "Yeah, Jay's not the problem. Don't worry about him," he said, glancing at Jason, who was leading Alyssa and Julianna out of the kitchen. "Sartelli, your dad's coming in a few?"

"Yeah, he should be here any minute," Bryan replied, eyeing Chris apprehensively. "We should find Jon and go wait outside."

Jon was easy to find. Of course, he had found a pretty girl to flirt with and hadn't left his spot by the refrigerator for an hour.

Chapter 16

Chantal lay across her queen-size bed, peering through tears at the scrapbook in front of her. Her bed was fully blanketed with photo albums, loose photos, and scrapbooks of her and Andy. Her leopard-print comforter was in a messy heap on the hardwood floor, and she lacked the motivation to pick it up. She was so tuned into her memories of Andy that she did not even notice her father enter her bedroom.

"Chantal, Jon's here to see you," he said. "Would you like me to send him in?"

Chantal looked up at her father in shock. "Jon? Jon Anderson? My Jon?! But it's midnight!" she exclaimed, throwing aside her scrapbook. "What ... what ... when did he get here?"

"Just a few minutes ago," her father replied. "He heard about Andy's accident and got worried about you. Do you want me to send him up?"

Chantal nodded. "Just give me a couple of minutes," she said while rising from her bed. As her father exited the room, Chantal began frantically tidying up her belongings. She couldn't believe Jon cared enough to come over in the middle of the night! Quickly, she pulled her messy hair into a ponytail and threw on her purple bathrobe. She had just enough time to wipe off the mascara that had run down her face before Jon knocked on her door.

"Hey," he said softly and entered her bedroom. "I, uh, just found out about Andy. How're you holding up?"

Chantal walked over to Jon and hugged him tightly. "Not so well," she replied as her eyes filled with tears. "Thanks for thinking of me."

"How could I not?" Jon asked, releasing Chantal from his embrace. "You are the first thing I thought of."

Chantal smiled slightly.

"Can we sit down and talk for a bit?" Jon asked, eyeing Chantal sympathetically.

She decided at that moment that his warm brown eyes could have melted a glacier. "Of course," Chantal replied, leading Jon over to her couch as her heart pounded heavily against her chest.

⸻◦✖◦⸻

Jon took a seat and looked affectionately at the only girl he'd ever loved. He hated seeing Chantal hurt and wanted more than anything to take away her pain. It was somewhat awkward for him to be alone with her because they had not had a private conversation in over a year.

"When the doctor told me he was in a coma, I almost lost it," Chantal admitted, hugging her knees to her chest. "The whole thing seemed surreal to me. It still does. He was just here with me yesterday, watching a movie on this couch."

"Tal, Chris came up with a really good idea tonight. Actually, he said he and Jay came up with it," Jon began. "Tomorrow, we are going to talk to Pastor Mark and see if we can arrange a prayer service for Andy."

"Really?" Chantal asked with her tone expressing how touched she was by the idea. She let out a deep breath as tears began pouring from her green eyes. "Thank you so much," she said and threw her arms around Jon.

"Hopefully the church will be able to do it on such short notice. We'll have to gather as many people as possible. Bryan is going to ask Courtney if her dad will spread the word. Chris, Jay, Bryan, and I are going to walk around tomorrow and tell everyone we see. Everyone knows Andy around here. He's like the golden child of Montgomery. I'm positive we could have a good-sized group gathered by tomorrow night," Jon explained, still holding Chantal in his arms.

"Tomorrow night!" she exclaimed, pulling free from Jon's arms. "That soon?"

"Well, we were afraid we might not have that much time," Jon said slowly, hoping his reasoning would not upset Chantal. "We weren't sure how Andy's doing?"

Chantal shrugged slowly. "I don't know either," she replied, looking down at her hands.

"So, we figured the sooner the better—just to be safe. Despite what you might think of me, I still believe strongly in the power of prayer," Jon said, looking warily at Chantal.

Chantal looked up at Jon strangely. "What do you mean 'despite what I think of you?'"

"I don't think it's the right time to talk about us, but I just want you to know that I believe Andy is in God's care," he stated seriously. "I haven't been to church in a long time, but I never stopped believing."

Chantal nodded and smiled slightly. "I know. I know you still have faith. I think you've just gotten a little lost."

Jon felt convicted by Chantal's words, but he knew she was right. Believing wasn't enough, not after having once been so close with God. Since Chantal broke up with him, Jon had felt empty inside. He had written it off as a consequence of losing their relationship, but for the first time, he realized the emptiness could stem from something deeper.

When Jon had dated Chantal, he never felt the need to be sexual with her. They had God in their relationship, and that was more fulfilling than any type of sexual act. Sex could not fulfill; Jon's relationship with Alyssa had proven that. At first, he had thought fooling around with Alyssa would make him happy, but he had quickly realized it didn't fill any of his emptiness. Even when he lost his virginity to her, he hadn't felt any better. Actually, he had felt much worse. Having sex with Alyssa had been disastrous to Jon's well being and to their relationship. He hoped Chantal thought he was still a virgin but realized what she thought wasn't what mattered most. God knew the truth, and Jon knew he needed to repent.

"Jon, are you okay?" Chantal questioned him. "You look really confused."

"Oh no, Tal, I'm fine," he assured her as he escaped from his contemplation. "I'm just looking forward to getting people together to pray. Andy and I aren't friends, but I still want what's best for him."

"That's really big of you," Chantal remarked. "I hope Andy would do the same for you if the situation were reversed."

"Um, knowing Andy, he would have already had the service arranged, and everyone would have gotten printed invitations in the mail this morning," Jon laughed.

Chantal's face fell. "He's such an amazing person," she said softly. "I really believe God can use him in this world for great things. I don't think He will let Andy die. I've been having a hard time dealing with the fact that if I'd let Lady in, this *never* would have happened. I found myself apologizing over and over again to my family, Andy's family, God, and myself. Then I remembered God works all things together for good to those who love Him. Andy and I love God, so I know whatever happens will be for the best."

"Romans 8:28," Jon said and smiled.

Chantal nodded. "Yeah, it's important for us to trust in God right now. He has a plan, and I know someday I'll look back and understand why all this happened."

"Chantal, your faith is inspiring," Jon said, taking hold of her right hand. "Here I thought you'd be coming apart at your seams. I should have known better."

Chantal shrugged. "I'm glad you came by. I wasn't sure if anyone knew what happened," she said softly.

"No one knew until tonight. Jason pulled Chris aside at the party and told him. Then Chris told Bryan and me on the way home," Jon explained.

"The party?" Chantal asked. "Why was Chris at Alyssa's party? Why were you?"

Jon rolled his eyes. "Long story, but don't worry. It wasn't Chris's idea."

"Do you feel like elaborating? I could use a good story to take my mind off Andy," Chantal said, again pulling her legs tightly to her chest.

"Sure. Well, earlier today I went to the mall with Courtney and Bryan," Jon began. "While we were there, we ran into Julianna and her mom. They were shopping for an outfit for Julianna to wear to Alyssa's party."

"Wait, what?" Chantal interrupted him. "Why would your girlfriend be invited to your ex-girlfriend's party?"

Jon laughed. "Your sister would be a better person to ask than me."

Chantal lowered her eyebrows and stared at Jon strangely.

"So, as you can imagine, I was surprised to learn that Julianna was going to Alyssa's party with Cathy instead of going to the movies with me, Chris, Marielle, Courtney, and Bryan," Jon continued. "Evidently your sister invited her to get ready with her."

"Julianna was at my house today?" Chantal questioned him in disbelief. "Why in the world would Cathy invite her over?"

"I'm pretty sure it had something to do with me," Jon replied. "I had such a pit in my stomach during the movie that I begged everyone to leave before it was over. Julianna is so naïve and insecure. I knew she was going to get sucked right into Cathy and Alyssa's world."

"They're like quicksand," Chantal said.

"So, I dragged everyone to the party, where I proceeded to confront Julianna," Jon explained. "She was intoxicated. She actually blew me off. Then she was inseparable from Alyssa for the rest of the night."

"Wow! I am shocked," Chantal stated. "I don't know Julianna that well, but I figured she had some commonsense. Courtney and Marielle must be upset. Julianna ditched you all for my sister. That doesn't make any sense."

"Well, I think Cathy and Alyssa wanted to come between Julie and me," Jon reasoned. "I'm sure they're still bitter about my breakup up with Alyssa. They're conniving like that."

Chantal's green eyes filled with tears.

"So, once again I lost someone I cared about to the partying scene," Jon sighed. "I think I figured out why it keeps happening to me, though."

"Because people are weak to temptation?" Chantal assumed.

"Well, that, too—I guess. That's no excuse, though. No, I think it keeps happening to me, so I'll understand how you felt when I did it to you," Jon said slowly, hanging his head. "I was insecure, just like Alyssa and Julianna. I gave into Chris's pressure right in front of your face. I started getting drunk and high at parties. I can't believe you stayed with me as long as you did!" Jon went on, unable to look at Chantal as he spoke. "Losing our relationship woke me up. That's why I shied away from everything else Chris, Jay, and Bryan began experimenting with. I actually started to resent them. For the past year, I've had no desire to drink at all. I wish I could go back to seventh grade and do everything all over."

He looked up at Chantal once he finished speaking. She was staring at him with a perplexed expression on her tear-glazed face. "I'm so sorry, Tal," he added. "I wasn't even in love with Julianna or Alyssa, and it still hurt to lose them. I can't imagine how much I hurt you."

Chantal swallowed deeply and sent Jon a questioning glance.

"I feel bad talking about this now, but I just need you to know that I'm sorry."

Chantal appeared stunned by Jon's confession. "Okay, wait ... back up," she said after a moment. "Nothing hurt worse than when you started going out with Alyssa. You replaced me in *one day*. How do you think that made me feel?"

"What are you talking about?" Jon asked, looking directly into her eyes. "You left a message on my answering machine saying that you were through with me. You even said I should go out with Alyssa."

"What?!" Chantal exclaimed loudly.

"So, I pretty much took that as a breakup," Jon stated matter-of-factly. "What else was I supposed to think?"

"Jon, I never said *anything* like that," Chantal shook her head in dismay. "I would never have told you to go out with someone else. I have been infatuated with you since sixth grade! You actually thought I said that?"

"Obviously," Jon replied flatly.

"Oh my gosh," Chantal heaved as her eyes grew wide.

"What?"

"Cathy left that message. She must have!" Chantal cried. "You know my voice. Did it really sound like me?"

"Well, yeah, pretty much."

Chantal's eyes widened with anger. "She thought you had developed feelings for Alyssa because you were spending so much time with her, and she really wanted me to break up with you. I bet she pretended to be me and left you that message."

"What?"

"I didn't leave that message, Jon. I swear. The only person it could have been is Cathy."

Jon eyed Chantal strangely, trying to process the gravity of what they were uncovering.

"After we broke up and you started dating Alyssa, Cathy became close with her," Chantal said. "I was devastated that Alyssa backstabbed me for you, so I shut them both out completely."

"Alyssa never backstabbed you," Jon said, shaking his head. "I called her the night we broke up to find out what had gotten into you. She said you had been shopping with her all day and that you hadn't called me once. If anything, Alyssa defended you."

"That doesn't make any sense," Chantal stated slowly.

"When you called me that night, I only said that I had to 'call my new girlfriend Alyssa' because of what your voicemail said," Jon explained. "Alyssa and I didn't hook up for months—not until you made it clear you were through with both of us. Even after you had it out with her, she was hesitant to go out with me. After losing you, I clung to her for support. She was my best friend, and I was heartbroken."

Chantal stared at Jon blankly.

"Are you okay?" Jon asked, placing his hand on her shoulder. "I didn't mean to upset you. I thought you already knew this."

Tears began pouring from Chantal's eyes. "See, all along I thought Cathy might have tried to break us up," she expressed, wiping tears from her face with her bathrobe. "I was certain Alyssa had been a part of it. After you told me she was your new girlfriend, I flipped out on her. I did not even give her a chance to explain. It hurt so bad to think my best friend had done that to me! Then Alyssa and Cathy became friends so quickly that I assumed it had been a scheme."

"Chantal, I am *so* sorry. I didn't mean for this to upset you. I don't even know how it came up," Jon apologized earnestly.

Chantal released her knees from her chest and leaned back against the couch. She sat, shaking her head from side to side, allowing tears to flow freely from her eyes.

"I feel like such a jerk. I never should have mentioned any of this. I came here because I was worried about you. I didn't mean to make you more upset," Jon said.

"No, I'm glad you told me all this," Chantal said after a moment. She turned towards him. "I can't believe I've been upset about something for over a year that didn't even happen. It kills me that I lost you for no reason. Poor Alyssa probably had nothing to do with it at all. No wonder she started acting so rebellious. She lost her best friend over something she didn't even do. I can't believe I was so stupid to never even talk to you about this. I didn't have any interest in hearing out you or Alyssa. I was so hurt that I just closed up."

"Well, I'm kind of sitting here feeling the same way. I've thought all along that you just didn't like me anymore. I actually thought you hated me and that was why you broke up with me. I could even understand why you would hate me. I wasn't being the best boyfriend in the world, and I certainly wasn't acting like the kid you started dating. After a while, it just made sense that you had broken up with me," Jon expressed.

"Well, maybe I would have if you had become any more like your friends," Chantal replied. "But I loved you so much. The thought of not being with you scared me worse than you tripping on acid."

"Chantal, I've never touched acid. I've never even smoked a cigarette, or eaten mushrooms, or anything," Jon stated. "If you hadn't broken up with me, I probably would have tried it all. Before I lost you, I thought keeping up with my boys was important. Then, like I said, I got my wakeup call. None of that stuff is worth anything to me, and it never was."

"So, what you're saying is that despite how manipulative Cathy can be, she actually brought some good into your life?" Chantal asked, smiling as she glanced at Jon. "Ironic, isn't it?"

"Well, I never would have looked at it that way," Jon said slowly, "but I guess, in a way, what happened was good for me."

"Well, you definitely took my mind off Andy for a while," Chantal laughed. "Good thing for Cathy I'm not vengeful."

"How can you not hate her?" Jon asked, shaking his head in disbelief.

"Love your enemies, bless those who curse you, do good to those who hate you, and pray for those who spitefully use you and persecute you," Chantal replied, smiling warmly at her first love.

Chapter 17

Saturday morning, Chris awoke at seven o'clock and hurried downstairs to eat breakfast. His mother was already up, having a cup of coffee at the kitchen table. She barely glanced up from her magazine when Chris said good morning to her.

Chris poured a bowl of cereal and took a seat across from his mother. Silently, he began praying for God to guide him through the day. He asked God to use him in whatever way He wished. He prayed that God would work through him and fill him with the Holy Spirit. He asked for strength, as he did every day, to resist temptation. He also prayed for Andy's recovery and for his family and friends' salvations.

"Why are you just sitting there?" Mrs. Dunkin asked, putting down her magazine and glancing strangely at her son. "Aren't you going to eat?"

"I was praying," Chris replied, looking directly into his mother's eyes. "Andy Rosetti is in the hospital. He got injured during the storm. He's in the ICU."

Chris's mother brought her hand to her lips in surprise. "Oh, I hadn't heard. That's terrible," she said, sounding more cordial than concerned.

"Today, Bryan, Jay, Jon, and I are going to try to put a prayer service together for him," Chris stated as he began eating his breakfast. "Bryan and his dad are going to be here in a half hour. We have to break the news to some people and then go to the church and make our request."

Chris's mother's jaw dropped. "What has happened to my son?" she asked, raising her perfectly shaped eyebrows.

Chris laughed and shrugged. "What do you mean?"

"Well, here you are up at 7:00 a.m. on a Saturday morning, praying at the breakfast table, with plans to organize an event at a church," his mother said as a smile spread across her darkly shaded lips. "I used to have to drag you out of bed for dinner."

Chris rolled his eyes. "Yeah, yeah, I know how useless I used to be."

"It's nice to see you doing something productive," his mother commended him.

"Thanks," Chris replied, surprised by her kind words. "Going to church has made my life so much better. I have such different desires now. I wish you and Dad would come with me sometime."

"Katie told me you quit smoking," his mother said, ignoring his invitation, "and drinking, and all the *other* things she hated you doing."

Chris blushed slightly and nodded. "Yeah, God straightened me out a bit."

His mother smiled. "Well, I think you've done a pretty good job yourself. Your father and I had begun to worry about you."

"I didn't do anything, Mom. It's all God working in me," Chris stated flatly. "I wanted to stop doing drugs for a while. I tried on my own, but I was just in too deep to get out. Then I developed a relationship with God, and He cleaned me up. I haven't touched a drug since."

"Interesting," his mother commented flatly.

"Well, Bry and his dad are going to be here soon. I have to finish getting ready," Chris said and stood up from the table. "I'll let you know if the service is going to be tonight. Maybe you could come?"

His mother crossed her arms and glanced up and down at her son. She shook her head from side to side and smiled. "I'm proud of you, Christopher," she said warmly. "Let me know what I can do to help."

⁂

Jason woke up early Saturday morning at Alyssa's house. He had spent the night in one of the guest rooms, as far away from his girlfriend as he could get. He assumed she had passed out in Alyssa's bedroom and hoped he could exit the house without catching a glimpse of her. Chris was going to be at Jason's house in two hours. The whole idea of talking to a pastor sketched Jason out, but in his heart of hearts, he wanted to believe in God. He certainly believed in helping out Andy and supporting Chantal.

Jason managed to escape from Alyssa's without being noticed. He arrived home twenty minutes later and began cooking breakfast. He decided to make enough banana pancakes for his entire family. After eating a few pancakes and cleaning up the kitchen, Jason hurried upstairs to get ready. He passed his father on the way to his bedroom and quickly mentioned the possible prayer service.

"I just hope that boy makes it," Jason's father stated as he shook his head from side to side. "It's a shame what happened to him. I'm just so thankful it wasn't you."

Jason smiled slightly and then hung his head. Despite Chris's comforting words the night before, Jason still wished he could have taken Andy's place.

"Good luck today, Jason. I'm sure you'll get a large group together," his father encouraged him while patting his shoulder.

"Keep your mother and me posted. We can make time to attend Andy's service. Matt and Luke will be there, too."

"Thanks Dad," Jason replied, hugging his father before heading off to his bedroom.

⁂

"What a nice surprise!" Courtney cried as she opened her bedroom door. The Angelettis' butler had kindly escorted Chris and Bryan to Courtney's suite, where Courtney and Marielle had been sound asleep.

"Wow, guys! What are you doing here?" Marielle asked, jumping off Courtney's king-size bed. "Didn't we just leave you a few hours ago?"

"Like eight or nine," Chris replied as he entered Courtney's tidy bedroom. He hugged Marielle so tightly that he lifted her off the floor.

"So, what's the deal? What are you guys doing here?" Courtney asked.

"Sit down, Court. We have something to tell you," Bryan said, leading Courtney over to her bed.

For the next half hour, Chris and Bryan explained what had happened to Andy. As expected, both Marielle and Courtney were shocked by the news and eager to help.

"We should go to the hospital right now and see him!" Courtney exclaimed. "We need to find out everything we can about his condition. Then I can see if there are any strings my dad can pull to help out his family. Andy needs to receive the best care possible."

"Yeah, shouldn't he be in Boston?" Marielle asked, placing her arms across her chest.

"Listen, Court, Marielle, we already have some things planned," Chris said. "Jay and I came up with an idea last night that will really help Andy. That's what we were talking about outside. Bryan and Jon are going to help us, and you are more than welcome to. We want to organize a prayer service for Andy at our church. We're going to Jason's at ten, and then we're going to see Pastor Mark. Andy's life is in God's hands now; there is nothing anyone can do for him that God can't. So, we plan on going around town and telling everyone we see. I thought maybe your dad could let some people know. I think we could get something good together by tonight."

Courtney and Marielle's jaws dropped.

"What's wrong with you guys?" Bryan asked, glancing from his girlfriend to Marielle.

"Nothing," Courtney replied quickly, "it's just that you guys hardly hang out with Andy. I can't believe you've already planned this whole thing out. I mean, it's awesome! I'm just kind of blown away. You said Jay helped you come up with the idea? *Jason* and *church*?"

Chris nodded. "Yeah, he's really worried about Andy. Jay's well-acquainted with Andy because of Cathy and Chantal."

"Doesn't Andy *hate* Jon?" Marielle asked, looking strangely at her boyfriend.

Chris nodded again. "That doesn't matter. Jon still wants the best for him. Jon and Jason are both pretty considerate people."

"I like Andy, but it doesn't matter if we're friends with him or not," Bryan spoke up as he grabbed hold of Courtney's hand. "We need to do all we can to help."

Courtney and Marielle looked at each other and smiled. "I'm so proud of you guys," Courtney said, reaching out to hug the boys. "You really believe in prayer."

"Whatever things you ask in prayer, believing, you will receive," Chris stated slowly.

Courtney shook her head in awe. "Was that just Chris Dunkin, quoting the Bible?" she laughed and playfully punched Chris's arm.

⁕

Alyssa woke up, sandwiched between Cathy and Julianna, on her queen-size bed. Immediately, two people crossed her mind: Andy and Chantal. She carefully climbed over Julianna, making sure not to wake her—although she was certain that Cathy and Julianna would be passed out for *quite* some time.

Shortly after Jason told her the news about Andy, Alyssa had made everyone leave her house. Only Cathy, Julianna, and Jason had been invited to stay the night. After everyone left, Alyssa and Jason had cleaned the house while Cathy and Julianna threw up in separate bathrooms. Alyssa knew Jason was at his wits end with Cathy, and Alyssa harbored similar feelings. She could not figure out how she had ended up being best friends with such a cold person.

After quickly throwing on a pair of boot-cut jeans, UGG boots, a hip-length sweater, and a thick belt, Alyssa ran down to the first level of her home. She had thought of calling Chantal but decided against it. After eating a breakfast bar and brushing her teeth, Alyssa made her way into the garage. Against the back wall was a bunch of junk that hadn't been used in years. That included her mountain bike, which was covered with cobwebs from handles to pedals. Pulling it out from behind a spare tire and a can of gasoline, she brushed the thick layer of dust off its seat. She smiled; Chantal's house was only a twenty-minute bike ride away.

⸻ ✥ ⸻

"Well, Jon, it is certainly nice to have you join us," Mrs. Kagelli greeted him as he took a seat at the dining room table that morning. Considering the circumstances, Jon's mother had allowed him to spend the previous night in the Kagellis' guest room.

"It's nice to be here," Jon replied, smiling at Mrs. Kagelli.

"Chantal was telling me that you and your friends are going to see Pastor Mark today about a prayer service for Andy. I think that is an excellent idea. God can do more for Andy than anyone

79

else," Mrs. Kagelli spoke as she scooped scrambled eggs onto everyone's plate. "Make sure to let us know the outcome of your talk. We should be up at the hospital most of the day. Call there if you need to reach us."

"I will," Jon said. "We're leaving from Jason's at ten. I'll have to leave soon to walk there."

"You're not walking there," Mr. Kagelli laughed. "We'll give you a ride on our way to the hospital. I am very familiar with Jason's house, and if it was close by, I would have a thousand less miles on my car."

"Thanks, Mr. Kagelli," Jon said, grateful for the Kagellis' hospitality.

Mr. Kagelli led them in grace and in a prayer for Andy's recovery. Jon noticed Chantal's eyes fill up with tears, and he tried hard to empathize with her. If Chantal loved Andy even a fraction of the amount Jon loved her, he knew she must be agonized. Mr. Kagelli concluded by asking God to place His hand upon Jon, Jason, Chris, and Bryan.

"Thank you," Jon said when Mr. Kagelli finished praying. "It will be nice to see Pastor Mark again," he added, regretting that he had not attended church in the past year and a half.

"I'm sure he will be happy to see you, too," Chantal said from across the table.

Sitting around the Kagellis' dining-room table brought Jon back to the happiest days of his life.

———※———

Chantal had just finished breakfast when she heard a faint knock on the front door. She watched as her mother answered the door and spoke with whomever was on the front steps. After a moment, her mother returned inside with Alyssa trailing behind her. Chantal widened her eyes and quickly looked down at her empty plate.

"Chantal, Alyssa came by to see you," Mrs. Kagelli said, placing her hands on Alyssa's shoulders. Chantal looked up and glanced strangely at Alyssa.

Alyssa swallowed deeply and glanced at the floor. "Jason told me about Andy," she said quietly, swaying her weight from foot to foot, "so I wanted to come by and see how you were doing." She looked up and made direct eye contact with Chantal.

A million thoughts began running through Chantal's mind. After her talk with Jon, Chantal's negative feelings toward Alyssa had dissipated. Before she had fallen asleep, she had prayed for an opportunity to reconcile with her old best friend.

Chantal rose out of her chair and slowly walked around the dining table. She hesitated only slightly before throwing her arms around Alyssa. "Thank you," she said, as she continued to embrace her. Tears began streaming down both girls' faces. "I'm sorry, Alyssa."

"I'm sorry, too," Alyssa sobbed, "and I'm so sorry about Andy."

Chantal pulled free from their embrace and glanced at her father. "Dad, do you think you could drive Jon to Jason's and then come back and get me? I really need to talk to Alyssa about something. Jon, do you mind?"

Both Jon and Mr. Kagelli agreed with ease to Chantal's request. Just when Chantal thought the situation couldn't get any more interesting, Cathy came stumbling through the front door. Her recently highlighted, blonde and auburn hair was up in a messy bun; her clothes were wrinkled; and her face was nearly colorless. She began hustling past the dining room and then stopped abruptly. She did a double take before dramatically dropping her jaw and widening her bloodshot eyes. Chantal had never seen her sister look so terrible.

"Wow! I walked around your house, looking for you, in fear you were in bed with my boyfriend, but it turns out you'd just gone to my house without me!" Cathy exclaimed, placing her arms across her chest. She shot her eyes from Alyssa to Jon and smiled. "Aww, just like old times, I see. Alyssa, Jon, and Chantal: the perfect love triangle."

Chantal stared at Cathy in disbelief. *You've got to be on some serious drugs,* she thought. Once upon a time, Cathy had been Chantal's closest friend. In less than two years, her personality had changed enough to make Chantal realize drugs had to be a factor, drugs beyond alcohol and marijuana.

"Okay, Cathaleen, in the living room—right now!" Mr. Kagelli demanded, yanking his caustic daughter into the room across the foyer.

Chapter 18

"Wow, I haven't been here in so long," Alyssa said as she walked into Chantal's bedroom. She twirled around and observed the room. It was exactly as she remembered it. The pastel green walls were lined with picture frames and collages. Stuffed animals and knickknacks were tucked into every nook and cranny. The beautiful olivewood cross from Chantal's grandmother still hung above her bed. The room felt as cozy and inviting as it ever had. "Aww, you still have our picture up?" Alyssa called out, moving across the room to the photo on Chantal's wall.

"Of course, I do," Chantal replied, taking a seat on her neatly made bed. When Alyssa sat down beside Chantal, she felt twelve years old again. She recalled the countless nights she had slept in Chantal's bed, staying up way past midnight, talking about boys. Alyssa had enjoyed those times, being innocent and acting her age.

"Alyssa, I need to apologize to you. Jon came over last night after he left your house, and we finally talked about our mess of a breakup. After putting our stories together, we realized we never meant to break up. More importantly, I realized it had nothing to do with *you*," Chantal began, looking directly into Alyssa's hazel eyes.

Chantal proceeded to explain everything to Alyssa: what Jon had thought, what she had thought, and what they had figured out. Alyssa had already known Jon's side of the story but was shocked to hear Chantal's. She was not surprised, however, to find out that Cathy had caused everything.

"I'm beginning to see through Cathy's sweet smile," Alyssa said, shaking her head. "I'm so sorry that you were hurt so badly. I can see how terrible it must have looked to you. You must have thought I had been after Jon from the start! I would have thought the same thing. I swear, Chantal, I never would have dated him if I knew you still loved him."

"I believe that," Chantal nodded, smiling slightly.

"Jon had been like a brother to me, for years. I never expected us to develop an interest in each other," Alyssa continued. "He was so heartbroken when he lost you. He clung to me because I was much more sympathetic than the rest of his friends. I felt so bad for him that I made comforting him my main priority. After a couple of months, he ended up expressing his gratitude to me ... and then ... well, he said he thought he was falling in love with me. I had no idea how to process that. Part of me thought he was rebounding, and part of me thought he was being sincere.

"I made a huge mistake, Chantal. Jon and I had an amazing friendship for close to a decade ... and ... well ... our friendship went down the drain with my virginity. He's so screwed up. After a while, I could understand why you broke up with him—well, you know what I mean. Jon wasn't acting like the good kid I had always known. He was selfish and bitter. He would get so angry, for seemingly no reason at all. One night, he and Jay almost got into a fistfight!" Alyssa exclaimed, widening her eyes. "The whole thing was Jon's fault, and everyone at the party knew it. Jon has been filled with anger ever since your breakup, and he has felt the need to let it out every chance he gets.

"I wish I never dated him. I would give anything to have my friendship back with him, and honestly, I'd give anything to have my virginity back. He doesn't deserve what I gave him. Once he had my heart, he trampled on it. I don't think he ever loved me. I'm not sure he has the capacity to love anymore."

"Oh, Lyss," Chantal said sympathetically. "I know Jon adored you. I know he cared about you. He just got really lost for a while. He got caught up following Chris and sort of lost himself. He knows he made a mistake. I'm sure he realizes that he hurt you. I think Jon has a lot of regrets and a lot of issues to work through."

"Maybe," Alyssa shrugged. She let out a heavy sigh and locked eyes with Chantal. "I should never have dated your ex-boyfriend, Chantal. I'm sorry. I know we hurt you. I know you had to see Jon and me together when we would come here with Cathy. It must have killed you. I'm not sure how you can be so forgiving, but I really appreciate it."

"For the last year and a half, I've been heartbroken, thinking Jon fell in love with you behind my back and that you sold me out for him," Chantal said. "When I found out the truth, it felt like a ton of bricks were lifted off my shoulders. I cannot believe how stupid I was to never hear either of you out."

"Well, during traumatic situations people tend to come together," Alyssa reasoned. "Jon and I care about you a lot."

"For some reason, I think this was all meant to be," Chantal said slowly. "It's like God allowed you and Jon to be taken out of my life, but He also knew this was going to happen to Andy. He put you two back into my life at the perfect time. It has cheered me up more than you can possibly imagine. If you had always stayed my best friend, then I would have nothing to be happy about right now. I would just be miserable about Andy and unappreciative of everything else."

Alyssa laughed. "Chantal, I love you!" she exclaimed. "You are the only person I know who could possibly see this situation that positively. I'm sitting here pissed at Cathy. Yet, she didn't break up with my boyfriend by pretending to be me, and she isn't my own flesh and blood! I really don't know how you can be so forgiving."

Chantal shrugged. "Sure, it hurts, but it's not worth staying upset over. I know everything happens for a reason, so what do I have to be upset about? If anything, I just feel intrigued by it all."

"Intrigued?"

"Well, yeah," Chantal said with a smile. "Like, why was it God's plan to take Jon out of my life? Neither one of us had planned on breaking up, so why did it happen? Jon told me last night that our breakup stopped him from trying drugs. So, right there I can see one reason. I'm sure more reasons will be revealed as time goes on. They always are. Most people would say they are coincidences, but I'm not that naïve. There is no such thing as coincidence or luck. It's really God working everything together as part of His plan."

"Well, I'm still mad at Cathy," Alyssa admitted with a laugh. "Maybe someday I'll be as spiritual as you, but until then, I'm going to think of all the reasons I have to kill her."

"Unforgiveness is like drinking poison and waiting for the other person to die," Chantal warned her. "If I had forgiven you and heard you out from the start, then I would have suffered much less this past year. You're going to feel like crap, holding bitterness inside you, and Cathy is going to feel fine. She isn't going to care whether you forgive her or not. You don't have to like her, but she's really not worth being upset over. It's your place to forgive her, God's place to heal your heart, and Cathy's place to repent."

"You're way too smart for a fifteen-year-old," Alyssa stated flatly. "Do you think I could come visit Andy with you? I told Jay I would help the guys out today, but I'm sure they will understand."

"Of course, you can!" Chantal cried. "I'd like all the support I can get. I seem strong, and then I look at Andy's expressionless face and break down. You would think I'd be out of tears by now."

"Aww, hun," Alyssa said, throwing her arms around Chantal. "Don't worry. You know he's going to pull through."

Chantal's eyes began filling up with tears. "Even if he does, the doctor said there is a chance he could have brain damage. I don't even know what I would do if that happened," Chantal said.

Alyssa widened her eyes as she released Chantal from her embrace.

"They said there is a good chance that even if he does wake up without brain damage that he won't seem like himself. He might not remember people—not even me or his parents," Chantal said. "The doctor also said he might need physical therapy. As of right now, we are just praying he wakes up."

Alyssa's eyes had begun filling with tears as Chantal spoke. The thought of Andy waking up and being mentally handicapped had never occurred to her. She couldn't imagine Andy being anything but charming, intelligent, and outgoing.

"I don't even want to think about the choice I would have to make if he has brain damage," Chantal admitted slowly, hanging her head. "I just want to be with him forever."

Chapter 19

Katherine awoke Saturday morning to the loudly ringing telephone. Reaching over Leslie, Katherine grabbed her phone off her nightstand. It was not even 10:00 a.m., and she could have used a lot more sleep. She, Leslie, and Lisa had been awake until 5:00 a.m., crying over Andy. Katherine had tried to get a hold of Bobby many times, but all her calls went unanswered. "Hello?" she said groggily into the phone.

"Hi, Kat. It's me," Bobby's smooth voice replied. "I'm so sorry I haven't called you in the past couple of days. I don't know if you heard, but Andy's in the hospital."

"Bobby!" Katherine exclaimed, sitting up straight. Her heart began pounding against her chest at the sound of his voice. "Hold on, I need to go out in the hallway. Lisa and Leslie are still sleeping," she said as she jumped over Lisa and ran out of her bedroom. "Sorry, they slept over last night and haven't had much sleep. We found out about Andy at Alyssa's party. I've been trying to get a hold of you ever since."

"Kat, I am so sorry that I haven't called. I feel like the worst boyfriend in the world," Bobby began, breathing loudly through the telephone into Katherine's ear. "I found out about Andy on Thursday night, and I was a mess. I just needed some time to be alone."

"Boyfriend?" Katherine questioned him, hearing nothing he said after that word. "You're not my boyfriend anymore."

"Huh?" Bobby asked. "Of course, I'm your boyfriend. What are you talking about?"

"You broke up with me on Thursday," Katherine stated flatly.

"Hun, I have no idea what you are talking about," Bobby stressed. "You hung up on me Thursday ... or we got disconnected because of the storm ... or something, but I wasn't breaking up with you. We were just talking about how football has been consuming all my time."

"I didn't hang up on you!" Katherine protested. "You hung up on me! You hung up right after you said you didn't want to go out anymore!"

"Kat, what are you talking about?" Bobby asked, sounding completely dumbfounded. "The last thing I remember saying is that I didn't want to go out for the team next season because I wanted more time with you. You sounded so angry that when I didn't hear a response from you, I thought you had hung up on me. But right after that, we lost our power, so I figured we had just gotten disconnected."

"Are you kidding me?" Katherine asked, feeling the color drain from her face. "I have been devastated for the last two days for no reason at all? You didn't break up with me?"

"Are you crazy? Why would I ever do that?" Bobby questioned. "I love you so much, Kat. You should know that by now."

"Well, all I heard on my end was that you didn't want to go out anymore, and then it seemed like you hung up on me," Katherine explained. "Then I tried to get ahold of you and couldn't, so I really thought you meant it."

"Wow. I can't believe you thought that. I am *so* sorry. I guess the phone cut out before it disconnected. Kat, all I want to do is give you a huge hug right now," Bobby expressed warmly. "I promise you, I had absolutely no intention of ending our relationship. All I want to do is make it better by not playing football next year. I just want you to be happy."

Katherine exhaled a heavy sigh of relief. "I don't care about you playing football! I'm just so happy you want to be my boyfriend! It was selfish of me to want you to quit football. I'm sorry, hunny. I can deal with it. I want you to play. I know you love it. I'm just so happy right now. Can you come over and give me that hug?"

"Of course. I already asked my mom to give me a ride to your house. I can be there in fifteen minutes. Okay?"

"Okay! Did you eat yet?"

"No. I haven't eaten since I found out about Andy."

"Okay, well, I'm going to start cooking us breakfast! You need to eat. I can't wait to see you! Love you! Bye!" Katherine exclaimed as she began bouncing down the nearby staircase.

"Love you, too," Bobby laughed.

Chapter 20

"Hi, Jon," Mrs. Davids greeted him as she opened the front door. "Jason's upstairs in his room. You can go on up. Chris and Bryan aren't here yet."

"Thanks, Mrs. Davids," Jon replied as he entered the two-story foyer. A twin set of stairs rose on either side of the room, joining together at a large landing. Five steps rose from the landing, connecting it to the second story of the three-story mansion. Jon ran up the stairs to the left of the foyer. At the top, he turned down the long hallway that led to Jason's bedroom. Jon tapped lightly on his door. Within seconds, Jason opened the door, pulled Jon into his room, and shut the door behind him.

"Dude, I'm so glad you're here first and not Chris," Jason said as he took a seat at his desk.

Jon sat down on Jason's bed and looked around the room. "Why? I thought you guys were cool?"

"Yeah, but I'm not done getting ready—if you know what I mean," Jason sniffled.

Jon darted his head in Jason's direction. "Dude, what are you doing?!" he exclaimed as his eyes widened in horror.

"Just bumping some Adderall," Jason replied before putting his head back down to a rolled-up dollar bill.

Jon widened his eyes. "I cannot believe you are snorting lines of Adderall before going to talk to my pastor!" he rebuked. He dropped his jaw dramatically as his heart began pounding against his chest. "Are you insane?"

"Dude, I do this all the time. It just keeps me focused," Jason replied. "It's not like I'm blowing lines of coke. I've yet to dabble with that substance, although I've had the opportunity."

"You are freakin' nuts!" Jon cried, shaking his head in dismay. "You're going to get yourself in trouble. That stuff was meant to be taken orally."

"You're starting to sound like Chris, who ironically is the only one of our friends who has dabbled with just about everything. Go figure."

Jon rolled his eyes. "Jay, he'll freak out if he finds out you're taking crap up your nose."

"Who do you think taught me how to do this?" Jason asked, raising his eyebrows. "Chris has blown a lot more than just Adderall."

Jon's stomach dropped. "Like what?" he asked and looked at Jason strangely.

"Come on," Jason sang dramatically while throwing his arms up in the air. "Do you really think he would have told you? You made it clear to us a long time ago that drugs aren't your thing—which is totally cool, by all means. But if you think Chris's drug problem stopped with weed, then you're just naïve. It's a freakin' miracle that he is straightedge right now. I don't get it. I don't get it at all."

Jon crossed his arms and stared at Jason skeptically.

"I just wouldn't want to tempt him by doing this in front of him," Jason said, as he crushed up another pill with his library card. "I respect his decision."

A loud knock on Jason's door broke through Jon's contemplation.

"Be right there!" Jason called loudly. He bumped another line of Adderall, wiped his nose with a tissue, threw his library card into his drawer, and headed for the door. "Where's Sartelli?" he questioned Chris after he opened the door.

"He's downstairs with Court and Marielle, talking to your mom," Chris replied, entering the room. "I just came up to get you guys."

"Nice," Jay sniffled and slapped hands with Chris.

"So, what are you on?" Chris asked immediately, letting out a heavy sigh and looking Jason up and down.

Jason laughed. "Just our old friend, Addy."

Chris shook his head. "Dude, you look messed up. We can't go to my church with you giddy like a little girl. You're an idiot."

Jason rolled his eyes. "C'mon, guy. I'm prescribed Adderall. It's not like I'm blowing lines of coke in my sister's bedroom or anything." He laughed and patted Chris on the back.

"Jay, you don't have a sister," Jon spoke up in confusion.

"Hey, look. I'm not proud of my past, but it doesn't need to be brought up right now," Chris stated sternly.

Jason closed his eyes and brought his hands to his forehead. "I'm sorry, dude. I'm wicked sorry," he said, still holding his head in his hands. "What the heck is wrong with me?" he muttered, throwing his hands down to his side. He walked across the room and slumped onto his bed.

"Jay, don't worry about it," Chris called out to his overly emotional friend. "I don't care if Jon knows. I don't care who knows. I'm not that person anymore. I'm actually glad you said that. It just makes the work God's done in my life clearer. Don't sweat it, Jay— seriously. I'm beyond caring at this point."

"You've tried coke?" Jon asked, looking up at Chris with disgust.

"Yeah," Chris nodded. "I was wasted sick one night, and Marc said it would sober me up. It worked, but I felt worse in the long run."

"Marc does coke?" Jon asked, raising his eyebrows in shock. Jon had known Chris's cousins for years; Marc had always been the most innocent one of the three brothers. He was co-captain of MLH's Varsity football team and in the homecoming court. While Taylor and Jordan continuously threw parties at Chris's house, Marc usually respected Chris's parents and avoided trouble. Jon had always looked up to Marc as someone with decent morals and a bright future.

Chris shook his head from side to side. "He definitely does *not* do coke. Marc stays away from drugs."

"That's what I thought. So, you must have been really messed up if he felt you needed to do that."

"I was an ambulance ride waiting to happen," Chris admitted.

"Well, I'm sorry, dude. I'm just really surprised," Jon said as he looked down at his feet. "I really thought you were above that."

"I definitely wasn't above that," Chris said flatly. "I tried everything I could get my hands on—Xanax, Adderall, molly, painkillers, mushrooms, acid—you name it. When that stuff wasn't available, I settled for weed or alcohol. I used to hate life when I was sober."

"I'm sorry," Jason stated, turning around on the bed to face Chris. "We agreed to never bring up what happened that night. You're right. I must be messed up."

"Jay, you don't need that crap," Chris said, taking a seat at Jason's desk. "I don't even think you have ADHD or whatever they thought you had when you were little. You're a straight-A student in level zero classes. You don't seem to have a problem paying attention. You need to start sleeping and stop depending on drugs for energy."

Jon sat on Jason's bed, glancing from Chris to Jason in

disbelief.

"Dude, are you okay?" Chris questioned Jon warily. "You look like your dog just died."

"I'm in shock," Jon replied defensively. "I can't believe you were *that bad,* Chris. Cocaine? Painkillers? You are my best friend, and you hid that from me? I can't believe you take stuff up your nose, Jay. I feel like I don't even know you guys!"

"Don't say that, dude. You know us. We just have some skeletons in our closets," Chris said. "Don't you see what's happening?"

"Um, yeah. I'm finding out some horrible stuff about my closest friends," Jon replied, glaring at Chris. "Next, I'll find out Bryan is a heroin addict or something."

Chris laughed. "Ha, yeah right. Bryan barely drinks anymore, let alone messes with illegal things. Courtney has him whipped to a chain. Don't start thinking bad thoughts. You've been a Christian a lot longer than me; you know how spiritual warfare works. This is just the devil trying to come between us, so we don't carry out our plan for Andy's prayer service. He's putting thoughts in all our heads to make us upset. I'm sure that is why Jay said what he did in the first place. You can't play into his trap," Chris stated, staring directly at Jon.

Jon sighed and looked away from Chris.

"You wouldn't normally say things to make me feel guilty," Chris added. "Guilt comes from Satan, not God. I've already confessed my sins, and God has forgiven me. Whenever you start to feel bad about something you've already been forgiven for, it is just the devil trying to condemn you."

"That's deep, guy," Jason said, sounding rather skeptical. He glanced from Chris to Jon. "Is that really true?"

It is, and it's so weird to hear Chris talk like this, Jon thought as he nodded, somewhat reluctant to admit that Chris was right.

"That's cool He forgives like that," Jason said nonchalantly.

Chris laughed. "Jesus suffered a gruesome, painful death so idiots like us wouldn't have to burn in hell. If He did that for us, how can you be surprised He'd forgive us? That was the entire point of what He went through."

Jason shrugged. "I have a hard time believing anyone would do that for me. I'm actually a pretty terrible person."

"People don't get into Heaven by being good people. A lot of people think that, but that's just one of the devil's best lies. According to God's standards, one sin alone would keep you out of Heaven. Sin separates us from God and deserves punishment. That's why Jesus died on the cross: to pay the penalty for our sins so we could be forgiven," Chris explained.

Jason stared blankly at Chris.

"Didn't they teach you that at St. Timothy's?" Chris asked. "You went there for eight years."

Jason shrugged. "Probably."

"Jesus paid the price," Chris repeated. "When you put your faith in Him, you are saved by grace, not by being a perfect person."

Jon blinked, realizing he had just witnessed Chris share the Gospel—something he had never thought would happen in a million years. "He's right," Jon spoke up, "and it's good for you to know that before you talk to Pastor Mark."

"Look, guys. I believe in God and everything, but I don't know *anything* about what you just said. I just want Andy to be okay," Jason said, as he stood up from his bed. "I'm sorry for taking Adderall before going to your church. I didn't mean to be disrespectful."

"Let's just head out," Chris said. "Sartelli and the girls must be getting impatient by now. Everything's cool though, right?"

"It's all good," Jason sang.

"It's cool," Jon stated, standing up to slap hands with his friends.

Chapter 21

Jason, Courtney, Bryan, Jon, Marielle, and Chris rushed through the front door of the church at eleven o'clock. The building was nothing like a typical church, architecturally. The size of it allowed for many activities to go on at once. The sanctuary was large enough to hold two thousand people comfortably. There were additional meeting rooms, Sunday School classrooms, an auditorium, offices, a kitchen, a nursery, and a bookstore.

Jason glanced around at the inviting atmosphere. Because he had attended a Catholic elementary and middle school, he had spent numerous hours inside churches. The formal ambiance had always left him feeling a bit tense. For that reason, Jason could never understand how Chantal, Courtney, and Chris felt comfortable spending so much time at church. However, the aura inside this building was different from any religious institution he had occupied.

"Let's see if Pastor Mark's in the office," Courtney called, taking lead of the group. "Hopefully he's here today."

"Shouldn't he be?" Marielle asked.

"Well, he has a lot to do each day, but one of the pastors is usually here," Courtney replied as she led them down a wide hallway.

"Hi, Rachel," Courtney greeted the secretary once they entered the small office.

"Well, hi, Courtney. Hi, Chris. Hi, kids," Rachel replied. "Mr. Anderson, it's nice to see you! How have you been?"

"I've been okay," Jon answered quietly, hanging his head as he spoke.

"Rachel, is Pastor Mark around?" Courtney asked, leaning on the counter-height desk.

"Mark is in a meeting right now. Jim is in his office if you'd like to see him," Rachel replied.

"We need to talk to Pastor Mark—I think. You see, our friend Andy was injured in the storm the other day, and he is in a coma. He's Chantal Kagelli's boyfriend. You know, Andy Rosetti?"

Rachel's jaw dropped. "Andy's in a coma? What happened?"

"He went to let Chantal's dog in, and the ceiling in the kitchen partially collapsed on top of him," Jason spoke up from behind Courtney. "The rest of us were downstairs in the basement. He's suffering from a severe head trauma."

Rachel grabbed ahold of Courtney's hand and immediately began praying for Andy's recovery. Chris and Jon bowed their heads in prayer, while Marielle, Bryan, and Jason glanced at each other uncomfortably.

"We want to see if Pastor Mark will hold a prayer service for Andy," Chris explained once Rachel finished praying. "Andy's well known in Montgomery, and we're sure people would come pray for him."

"I think that's a wonderful idea," Rachel said, wiping tears from her eyes. "I'm sorry for tearing up. My heart just breaks for his family."

"It's okay. We've all done our share of crying," Jason said compassionately. "Chris and I figured the best thing we could do for

Andy and his family was get people together to pray. I don't even go to church, and I think it's important. So, I'm sure everyone else will, too."

"What's your name?" Rachel asked, glancing at Jason with a friendly smile.

"Jay," he replied. "Jason Davids."

"I've heard your name before," Rachel said, staring at him in deep thought.

Jason blushed. He could only imagine what Cathy's family had said about him. *Oh, our daughter was a great kid until she met her loser boyfriend. Now she gets arrested, skips school, and smokes pot.*

"Weren't you the one who got that award last year?" Rachel asked suddenly. "Yeah, it was you, right? Michael Kagelli told me. You date his daughter, don't you?"

Jason nodded, eyeing Rachel nervously.

"Michael said you got an award for having the highest GPA at St. Timothy's Middle School," Rachel recalled, smiling warmly at Jason. "That's a great achievement."

Jason stared blankly at Rachel. He could not believe Mr. Kagelli had spoken highly of him, nor could he believe Rachel had bothered remembering such useless information. "Thanks," he said and dropped his blue eyes to the floor.

"All right. I'm going to interrupt Mark and tell him about what happened to Andy," Rachel announced while standing up from her desk. "I'll let him know you're here. You can take a seat in the waiting area."

"Thanks," Courtney said with a smile and then turned around to face her friends.

"Good thing you came with us, Court," Chris said once Rachel left the room. "I wouldn't have been comfortable talking to her like that. I'm surprised she remembered my name. I only met her once."

"Being the mayor's daughter gets me a lot of recognition, but people here really care about others," Courtney replied.

"I can see that," Jason said. "That Rachel lady seems awesome. No wonder Chantal and her parents are so nice. They're always here."

"Here is a good place to be," Chris remarked.

⁕

Alyssa stood beside Chantal over Andy's hospital bed. After three days in a coma, Andy had not made any improvement. The doctor had told Andy's parents that the longer Andy remained in a coma, the greater the risk was that he'd have brain damage.

Alyssa could not believe that Jason had been the one to tell her about Andy's condition. When she had spoken with Cathy on Friday, she had said nothing about Andy. Alyssa was surprised by both Jason's concern for Andy and his anger toward Cathy. In Jason's opinion, Cathy had gone one step too far. Alyssa found herself in complete agreement with him.

After hearing about Jason and Chris's idea for the prayer service, Alyssa had realized something crucial: she had been wrong for viewing Jason as the root of evil in their clique. Jason cared about other people. He was sensitive enough to cry in public. Cathy looked like an icicle next to him. Alyssa could not believe it had taken her so long to see Cathy's true colors. If anyone was the root of evil in her group of friends, it was, without a doubt, Cathaleen Kagelli.

Chapter 22

"Hi, Courtney," Pastor Mark greeted her as he walked into the waiting area. "I'm sorry to keep you all waiting. I am very concerned about Andy."

"Pastor Mark, these are my friends Bryan, Chris, Marielle, Jason, and you already know Jon," Courtney said as she gestured toward each of her anxious friends. Courtney briefly explained to Pastor Mark what had happened to Andy. "We were wondering if you could hold a prayer service here at the church for Andy? We think everyone's prayers would really help him."

"I think that's a great idea, Courtney," Pastor Mark said.

"Actually, it was Chris and Jason's idea," Courtney informed him. "I'm just the messenger."

"I know we have marriage ministry scheduled for tonight, but the sooner we can arrange this for Andy the better," Pastor Mark stated. "Why don't I go make some calls and see what I can do? I will get in touch with some of the other pastors and elders. Andy is a great kid. It's hard for us to understand why things like this happen, but we have to remember not to lean on our own understanding. I would like to get ahold of the Kagellis. I can imagine they are very upset. I'm sure they could use some prayer as well."

"They're at the hospital," Jon said. "I have the number if you'd like to give them a call. I talked to Chantal earlier, and her spirits were high. She has a lot of faith. She amazes me."

"She amazes us all," Jason spoke up as he leaned forward in his chair. He rested his chin on his fist and looked up at Pastor Mark. "If you talk to her, don't let her tell you it was her fault. I was there, and I know firsthand that Chantal did nothing wrong. Cathy can be pretty mean sometimes. She tried to blame Chantal for letting the dog out. Actually, it's just as much my fault as it is Cathy's. We went outside with Lady, without good intentions, and completely forgot about her."

Pastor Mark stared at Jason curiously. "Well, I'm sure your intention was not to leave the dog outside in a storm. Obviously, it was a mistake. Don't beat yourself up too much."

Jason sighed and put his head down. "We went outside to get high, sir. We were too baked to remember Lady had come outside with us."

Chris's eyes grew wide at the sound of Jason's words. *How could he admit something like that to a pastor? How does that make us look?* Jason hadn't even told Chris he had been high.

"When I look back at all the things I did at your age, I can't even fathom what I was thinking. I can't hate myself for my past. Jesus has wiped my slate clean with His sacrifice. I grew up in the seventies. When I was your age, I had my hands on every drug in sight," Pastor Mark said, glancing at Jason.

Jason quickly looked up at Pastor Mark.

"No matter why you feel responsible for this happening to Andy, you are not responsible," Pastor Mark stated sternly, staring directly into Jason's eyes. "God has allowed this to happen. All you can do is trust Him, repent, and pray."

Jason remained speechless.

Courtney smiled at her pastor. "Thanks for sharing that," she said. "I think you've helped more than you realize."

"I'm going to go make those calls. Why don't you check back with me in an hour or so? You can call the office or come back, whichever is easier," Pastor Mark said.

"Do you guys want to go to my house for lunch?" Courtney offered, glancing at her friends. Everyone except Jason seemed excited by the idea of food. Jason looked disturbed and distracted, as if he hadn't even heard Courtney speak.

"Lunch sounds good to me!" Jon exclaimed, jumping up from his chair.

"Okay, Pastor Mark, we'll call you in an hour," Courtney said as she stood up. "Thank you so much."

"Anytime, Courtney," Pastor Mark replied, waving goodbye to them before turning down the hallway to his office.

Chris, Courtney, and their friends had begun walking out of the office when Jason suddenly stopped and yelled, "Wait! Pastor! Can I talk to you?"

Chris watched in bewilderment as Jason ran after Pastor Mark. He knew that Jason felt bad about what happened to Andy, but he never expected him to run into a pastor's office.

"Rachel, could I make an appointment with Pastor Mark?" Chris asked as he walked over to her desk. After hearing that Pastor Mark had a history with drug abuse, Chris thought he could benefit from talking to him.

"Sure," she replied. "When would be good for you?"

"Any day after school," Chris said, deciding he could miss football practice if needed, "or some night this week. Maybe Wednesday after Bible study?"

"Okay, Wednesday it is," Rachel said and jotted Chris's name in the appointment book. "You know, I couldn't help but overhear what happened with your friend Jason. He might be lost right now, and I'm sure you're worried about him, but I see something special in him. Once in a while people come into this office, and I just get a feeling that God has a special call on their life."

Chapter 23

Later that afternoon, Bobby, Katherine, Lisa, and Leslie walked through the door of Andy's hospital room. They all looked surprised to see Alyssa sitting beside Chantal but said nothing about it.

Bobby moved close to Andy's hospital bed and stared blankly at his best friend's seemingly lifeless face. A feeding tube had been inserted into Andy's side. He was hooked up to five or six different monitors. The beeping from the machines drilled through Bobby's eardrums. He could not believe the doctors thought Andy might not survive the weekend.

Andy had been Bobby's very best friend since they were young. The thought of Andy not being by his side at graduation or at his wedding brought tears to Bobby's eyes. He found it extremely difficult to fight off the tears, but he knew he had to stay strong for the girls. For someone who had already lost so many people dear to her, Lisa was the epitome of a strong person; even she was falling apart.

"How long are we supposed to wait for him?" Jon asked as he and his friends sat in the church office. "So, much for lunch."

Courtney sighed. "Well, he's been in there for an hour already. Maybe you should go check on him, Chris?"

Chris raised his eyebrows at Courtney.

"What? You're best friends with him!" Courtney exclaimed defensively. "Jason's not even my friend. I'm not going in there!"

Chris rolled his eyes. "I've hardly talked to him in two months, and I don't even know Pastor Mark. Jon, why don't you go check? You're the one so eager for lunch. Maybe Jason will tell you not to wait for him."

Jon sat silently with his arms crossed, leaning back in his chair. Although lunch sounded wonderful, the idea of being somewhat personal with his pastor hurled his stomach into nausea. Even Rachel's friendly greeting had convicted Jon of his backslidden state. He didn't want to imagine the amount of guilt he would feel if he talked to Pastor Mark. Between being concerned about Andy, confused about Chantal, and upset about Julianna, Jon decided he felt enough emotions at once; adding guilt to the list could easily send him into a state of psychosis.

"I could go check on him," Bryan offered. "I've just been sitting here. I could at least do that."

"Have fun," Jon said sarcastically. "Jason's as emotional as he's ever been. I think all the drugs have turned him psychotic."

Bryan laughed. "Well, maybe he's always been psychotic, but we just didn't realize because he's always been on drugs."

"Whatever," Jon muttered and glanced at the floor. Despite his inner turmoil, Jon realized Jason's meeting with Pastor Mark was an answer to his own past prayers for Jason. Jon remembered coming to church multiple times a week—for years—taking blow after blow of ridicule from Jason. In seventh grade, Jon had prayed diligently for Jason's heart to be softened. Two years later, Jon sat with irritation, hoping Jason would keep his conversation with Pastor Mark short. Jon shook his head from side to side, wondering how his own heart had grown so hard. Two years ago, he would have given anything to see Jason meet with his pastor. He sighed, realizing he was far from the concerned friend he had once been.

"You're probably right, Jon," Chris said. "He's almost as bad into stuff as I used to be. I'd rather leave him alone and let him talk to Pastor Mark as long as he needs to."

"Why don't we wait for Jason and let everyone else go to Courtney's?" Marielle suggested.

"That's fine," Chris agreed. "Don't feel like you guys have to stay. I don't mind waiting for him at all."

"I think that's a really good idea," Bryan stated as he tugged restlessly on the sleeve of his shirt. "I have to admit, I'm going stir crazy right now."

"Fine. We can walk back to my house. I'll ask my mom to pick you guys up when Jay's done," Courtney said, glancing at Marielle and Chris for their approval.

"Whatever," Chris shrugged.

"We'll call your house once Jason's done," Marielle said with a smile. "I'm sure they're talking about Andy. Jason seems more concerned than anyone."

"All right. See you guys in a bit," Courtney called and motioned Bryan and Jon toward the exit.

Lisa ran out of Andy's hospital room, unable to catch her breath. Seeing Andy hooked up to numerous machines reminded her of the last day she had seen her father alive. Her father, whom she had loved more than anyone, had died after three days in a coma. Now, Andy—the person who had been her rock through all of her loss—was facing the same challenge. Lisa would not have gotten through middle school if Andy had not been there to cheer her up, wipe away her tears, and help her focus on her schoolwork. Moreover, Andy had introduced her to Jeff—the boy she wanted to spend the rest of her life loving. Lisa owed so much to Andy. The thought of never being able to thank him or hug him sent her slender body into dry heaves.

⁓⁂⁓

At the sound of heavy footsteps heading in his direction, Chris shot his eyes up from the floor. Within seconds, Jason entered the waiting area—appearing anxious, emotionally broken, and exhausted.

"Where's everyone else?" Jason asked, darting his reddened eyes back and forth.

"Having lunch at Courtney's," Chris replied, gazing at Jason with concern. "Is everything all right?"

"I don't want to talk about it," Jason snapped. "Let's just meet up with everyone and start telling people about the service. It's on for seven o'clock tonight."

Chris dropped his jaw.

"That's great news!" Marielle exclaimed, jumping up from her seat with excitement. "I can't wait to tell Chantal!"

Chris nodded and smiled. "You did all right, guy," he said, standing up to give Jason props.

"I had nothing to do with it," Jason said, shaking his head. "Pastor Mark called off marriage ministry and asked the other pastors to help gather people together. He's an amazing guy. Seriously, you would think Andy was his own son or something."

"We told Court we'd give her a call," Chris said, walking over toward Rachel's desk. "Should they come meet us here or should we head over there?"

Jason shrugged. "See what she wants us to do."

In fifteen minutes, Courtney and her mother arrived at the church. She said her father was going to make a special announcement on the local TV and radio stations. She said he agreed to notify all town officials about the service as well. Andy had been

107

actively involved in the community for years, so Mayor Angeletti said he was anticipating a big turnout. Courtney, Chris, and their friends had one job left to do: split up and tell everyone in town where to be at seven o'clock.

Chapter 24

Jason remained in complete silence as he followed Courtney through her massive home and into her bedroom suite. Before leaving the church, Marielle had called the hospital, learning that Alyssa was there with Chantal. Jason found the news interesting. He couldn't help but wonder what Cathy was up to. In his opinion, she should have been visiting Andy. Jason had a lot of lifestyle changes to make, and there was a big chance his relationship status was going to be one of them.

"So, we got ahold of Lisa, Katherine, Leslie, Adam, Jeff, and Bobby," Jon said, the second his friends walked into Courtney's bedroom. "They're going to spread the word about the service. I think we're in good shape."

"Nice," Chris commented, taking a seat beside Marielle on Courtney's leather couch. "Where's Bryan?"

"He's out on the balcony," Jon replied, pointing to the sliding glass door.

"You have a balcony, Courtney?" Jason exclaimed as his blue eyes grew wide with disbelief. "That's sick! Geez, you *are* spoiled."

Courtney laughed. "You can go check it out if you want. There's a nice view."

"Sweet," Jason said and walked across her room to the sliding glass door. As he stepped onto the granite balcony, he became amazed by the view of Montgomery.

"What's up, Jay?" Bryan called from the left side of the balcony. He looked comfortable, sitting in a lounge chair with his feet perched up on the railing, smoking a cigarette. Bryan rarely smoked, so Jason assumed he was a mess over Andy.

"I just had the most in-depth conversation of my entire life. What a day, huh?" Jason said as he sat down on the chair next to Bryan. He leaned back and closed his eyes, wishing Pastor Mark's words would stop running through his mind. He knew he should be more worried about Andy than himself, but his mind was stuck in overdrive. He also knew he needed to take Pastor Mark's advice if he ever wanted to feel normal again.

Lately, his emotions had been out of control. He had more mood swings than a woman going through menopause. He had tried to blame his moodiness on his relationship with Cathy, but after some reflection, he realized his irritability was probably causing some of their relational issues. In the past year, he had smoked weed and abused Adderall daily, drank most weekends, dabbled with Xanax and Vicodin, and tripped a couple of times each month. His problem was, without a doubt, drugs.

Jason breathed deeply, opened his eyes, and looked over at Bryan. "Give me one of those nasty things," he said and pointed to Bryan's cigarette.

Bryan laughed. "What, dude? You don't smoke!"

"Whatever," Jason shrugged and reached for a cigarette. "I need to smoke *something* instead of weed," he said, eyeing the cigarette cautiously and then putting it down on his lap. "I have to stop smoking weed. When I talked to Courtney's pastor, he told me everything I didn't want to hear, but everything I needed to. I need to lay off drugs."

Bryan glanced at Jason skeptically. He had never expected to hear those words come out of his mouth. Jason had made fun of Chris daily for turning straightedge. Jason smoked pot every morning before homeroom. Jason loved drugs.

"My emotions have been whack," Jason admitted. "I can function every day off of two hours of sleep. That's it. That's all I need. When someone only needs two hours of sleep, they should realize they have a *problem*. If I hadn't been high on Thursday, then I would have remembered Lady was outside. Don't you get it, Bryguy? None of this would have happened to Andy. Also, if I hadn't been high, *I* would have gone outside to get Lady when we realized she was missing. I just sat there like an idiot because I was stoned. Now, Andy could *die* because I have a drug problem."

"Wow, Jay, that's huge," Bryan said, glancing at his friend with concern. "Are you saying Court's pastor told you it was your fault?"

Jason shook his head quickly from side to side. "No, not at all. He told me exactly what Chris said. You know, that it's God's will, and there is a reason why it happened. He said that feeling convicted for doing drugs is good, but I shouldn't blame myself for what happened."

"Hmm," Bryan said quietly. "I agree with that."

Jason shrugged. "So, hopefully I'll be able to sleep someday like a normal person. I figure I can just take Adderall orally when I need to study. Plus, without you, Jon, or Chris getting wasted with me anymore, it's hardly any fun. The only person who likes taking drugs with me turned out to be Satan. Oh, and did I mention, I'm dating her?"

"Ha," Bryan laughed and tossed his cigarette over the railing.

"I don't know how long we're going to last," Jason stated, handing the unlit cigarette back to Bryan. "I heard smoking cigarettes makes it easier to give up pot, but I can't bring myself to do it."

"Good," Bryan stated flatly. "I've been trying to quit all year. I gross myself out, let alone Courtney."

"Don't be hard on yourself, guy. Anything's better than what I've been doing lately."

"Well, I'm here if you need anything. Just let me know," Bryan said as he stood up from his chair.

Although Jason had always been a good friend with good intentions, Bryan found his words hard to swallow. Whether Jason would admit it or not, Bryan knew he was addicted to Adderall—and, at that point, possibly Vicodin. Despite his concern, Bryan had not mentioned Jason's dependency to anyone. Jon and Chris knew nothing about Jason bumping Adderall on a daily basis. They had no clue that for the past month he had been popping Vicodin like they were Tic Tacs. Jon and Chris had no idea what Jason had been up to, and Bryan had no idea how to help him. The fact that Jason had been smoking weed since he was thirteen seemed like a much smaller problem than his prescription drug habit. Bryan knew that someone so dependent on drugs could not just stop on a dime. Jason needed rehab or a miracle as soon as possible.

Chapter 25

Bryan stepped into Courtney's bedroom from the balcony and glanced uneasily at Chris. "You need to go talk to him," he said, shaking his head from side to side. "He's having some sort of breakdown."

Chris raised his eyebrows and took a deep breath. "Why don't you guys head out? Jay and I will catch up with you," he suggested, glancing at his friends for their approval.

"Do you really think it's the right time for this?" Courtney asked, peering skeptically at Chris. "I think Andy should be our number-one priority."

"Well, I'm sure Jay could wait," Bryan said. "We *do* need to tell everyone about tonight. Even if Leslie, Katherine, and Lisa cover the lake, we still have a lot of Montgomery to cover."

"Bobby, Jeff, and Adam said they would take Sterling," Jon said. "So, that leaves us to cover Hamilton and downtown."

"You guys go ahead and start walking around Hamilton. I know God wants me to stay and talk to Jason," Chris stated firmly.

"How do you know He's telling you to stay?" Marielle asked, eying Chris skeptically.

"I pray every day for your eyes to be opened," Chris said after a short pause. "If you ask God to reveal Himself to you, He will. If you accept Christ as your Savior and ask to be filled with the Holy Spirit, you will be, and then you will know what it is like to hear God's voice. He speaks with a gentle tug on your heart. I can't really articulate it. I just hope, someday, you experience it for yourself."

Marielle looked perplexed by Chris's words. He knew time was of the essence, so instead of elaborating, he stepped outside onto the balcony. Jason quickly turned and faced the other way when he spotted Chris. He let out a heavy breath and hung his head. Then he placed his hands on the back of his neck and continued to breathe deeply.

Chris walked past Jason and took a seat to his left. He sat in silence for a moment, asking God to give him the right words to speak. "I'm sure you didn't like hearing what Pastor Mark had to say today," he began, swallowing nervously, "but I'm sure it was everything you needed to hear. Whatever he said to you, I know was said out of concern. Whatever may seem impossible right now is not impossible. Look at me, Jay. Look at me now and think about who I was three months ago. Can't you see how different I am? I didn't get where I am today on my own."

Jason lifted his head and turned toward Chris. "I know what I need to do," he said and rested his chin on his fist. "I need to stop taking drugs and start facing reality."

"You're missing the big picture," Chris stated matter-of-factly. "Why do it the hard way? I tried a bunch of times and failed. I couldn't get sober until I realized something greater: drugs were just one problem area of my life, and if I successfully gave them up, I would still be left with a ton of other problems. Remember the Fourth of July at Jon's beach house?"

Jason nodded and leaned back in his chair.

"Do you remember how I made you introduce me to Courtney?" Chris asked.

"Yeah, which was wicked awkward because she was there with Bryan. I didn't know you were going to ask her out a week later," Jason groaned.

"I was drawn to Courtney because I saw strength in her that amazed me," Chris said. "If you are sitting here wondering where I got the strength to straighten out my life, then you are feeling the exact same way I felt at Jon's party. I needed to get close to Courtney because I desired her strength.

"After she let me down, I got discouraged and fell right back into my old ways. Then, to my surprise, she shed light on the situation. I had gone after the wrong person all along. It wasn't *Courtney* I had been attracted to; it was God. I had thought spending time with her would give me strength, but I was wrong. I should have been spending time seeking God. After a month with Courtney, I hadn't grown any stronger, but once I found God, I felt whole."

"You're unreal right now," Jason scoffed and shook his head.

"I am happy leading a sober life. I'm learning to tackle challenges that I used to copout on by getting high. I don't need a substance to numb my pain or enhance my mood anymore. The high I get from seeing God at work in my life and inside me is better than any high I ever got from drugs."

Jason let out a heavy breath.

"Jay, it's me. *You know me,*" Chris pressed. "You know me better than anyone does. You know what drove me to get messed up in the first place. You know where my pain stems from. I found a better cure than drugs or alcohol."

Jason sighed.

"If your dad gave you a six-hundred-page book filled with promises for a happy, peaceful, and fulfilling life, would you ignore it?" Chris asked. "No way. You would read it and hold him to every single promise. I just don't understand why you won't read a book of promises from God."

Jason stared at Chris blankly for a moment and then stood up. "We should go tell people about the service," he said and began walking toward the slider. "It's almost three o'clock. We only have four hours."

Chapter 26

Alyssa left the hospital with Chantal around four o'clock that afternoon. She had been surprised by Chantal's sudden request to leave. Chantal had given no explanation but insisted on going home.

"I can't believe Cathy didn't come visit Andy," Chantal said sadly as they walked down the sidewalk. "Her support would have meant a lot to me."

"I wish I could make sense of her thought process for you," Alyssa said, glancing sympathetically at Chantal. "Even after hanging out with her for a year straight, I can't fathom what controls her mind sometimes."

"I don't get it. We used to be so much alike," Chantal said. "After she met Jason, she turned into a completely different person; yet I don't even think it's his fault. I actually think she's a bad influence on him."

"I think Jay has a big heart, but he hides it behind his humor," Alyssa commented. "He's not happy with Cathy either. Last night, he helped me clean my house while Cathy puked in the bathroom. He was going to walk home, just so he wouldn't have to sleep under the same roof as her, but I convinced him to stay in our guest room."

"Wow. Jason's usually really patient with her," Chantal said and glanced at Alyssa. "Doesn't he usually hold her hair back?"

Alyssa shrugged. "He has in the past, but she doesn't throw up that often. I really think she was on something last night. She looked horrible this morning, and for her to get that sick from a couple of strawberry daiquiris and a few shots is unlikely."

"I'm sure she smoked pot. Isn't that her forte?"

"That wouldn't make her nauseous," Alyssa replied. "She's gotten into worse stuff than weed and alcohol."

"Like what?"

Alyssa shrugged. "I'm not quite sure. I've seen Jason crush up pills and snort them. In my opinion she is just as bad as him, so I imagine she's done the same."

Chantal shook her head sadly from side to side. "They're only fifteen. Can you imagine what they're going to be doing by the time we're seniors? Maybe that explains why she's been acting so crazy lately. My poor parents. They caught her smoking twice this month, and I know they're still upset about her arrest."

"Cathy doesn't even smoke," Alyssa stated, shaking her head. "She just does it sometimes to make Jason and your parents mad, but she actually hates it. She does it way less than the rest of her friends—well, except for Jason."

"And Jon," Chantal added. "He doesn't smoke either."

"Right, but he's *not* Cathy's friend," Alyssa said. "Tell your parents not to worry about Cathy smoking. It's an act. She's just trying to get under their skin."

"Well, grounding her for a month after Jason's party did absolutely nothing for her character," Chantal sighed. "I just hope she hasn't gotten addicted to anything. That's really sad that Jason's taking things up his nose. He could screw up his life so easily. I don't understand why he would risk that."

"I don't think he takes it seriously. He sees what Luke and his friends do and just thinks it's normal to party hard. Plus, he and Chris were always inseparable. If you look at all the stuff Chris used to do, then it makes what Jason does not look so bad. Even though Chris and Jon went straightedge, Jason still has Cathy, Jeff, Lisa, Leslie, and his brother's crew to party with. Everything Jason does seems normal to him because of who he hangs out with."

"Lisa hides her imperfections well," Chantal commented dryly. "I know Andy wants me to become closer with her—and the other two—but I can't bring myself to do it. Katherine seems nice, but Lisa and Leslie ... well, I know you're friends with them, so I'm not going to say much ... but you know how they are. It bothers me how weird Andy acts around them. He's normal around Bobby, Katherine, and Adam, but he gets cocky around Leslie, Jeff, and Lisa."

"It must be hard to have a boyfriend with a completely different set of friends than you," Alyssa said. "I've seen Andy talk to Chris and Bryan in school. It seems like he tries to make an effort with your friends."

Chantal nodded. "Yeah, but you know Andy; he's friends with everyone."

"Except Jon!" the girls exclaimed in unison.

"He's always afraid I'm going to leave him for Jon—like I have the option," Chantal added.

"Chantal," Alyssa laughed, "you definitely have the option. Jon loves you."

Chantal rolled her eyes. "He used to a *long* time ago. There's a big difference."

Alyssa shook her head. "You don't see it, but everyone else knows you're still on his pedestal."

Chantal turned toward Alyssa and blushed deeply.

By five o'clock, Bryan, Courtney, Marielle, and Jon had finished telling everyone they saw in Hamilton about Andy's service. Courtney had been the spokesperson most of the time since everyone in Montgomery knew she was the mayor's daughter.

"I hope Chris and Jason catch up with us. We didn't even make a plan to meet anywhere," Jon said as they walked past Chris's street.

"They knew we were going to be in Hamilton, so maybe they headed downtown," Bryan suggested. "Unless they're still at Court's."

"I don't understand Jay's problem," Marielle complained. "Chris dropped everything for him. I thought this whole prayer service was their idea in the first place? Now, they're nowhere to be found."

"Don't doubt your boyfriend," Courtney said. "Jason is in good hands with Chris. I think that's what he needs right now. He's a mess. Chris has learned to pray before making decisions. I don't even do that as often as I should. With God guiding him, he's being more productive than we are. We're just doing what we want to do."

Marielle glanced strangely at Courtney and put her head down. "I really don't get you guys," she admitted quietly.

"You don't believe," Courtney stated matter-of-factly, "so you wouldn't get it."

"Well, I believe in God," Marielle said and looked up at Courtney. "I just don't know much about Him. My mother never raised me with religion."

"You're old enough to learn on your own," Courtney said flatly. "I'm not trying to give you a hard time, but I'm not going to let you blame your mother. After seeing the change in your boyfriend, of course you believe. But what do you believe?"

"I don't know. I told you I don't know anything about God," Marielle replied, pausing next to her. "Why do you care so much?"

"Because you're missing out," Courtney said matter-of-factly. "I want you to enjoy the blessings God has for you. I don't want you to settle for anything less than that."

"Thanks, Court," Marielle said slowly, "but I can't just devote my life to someone I can't even see."

"Marielle," Jon spoke up, "how can you recognize someone if you don't know what they look like?"

"What?" she asked, appearing caught off guard.

"You'd be able to see God in your life if you knew what He looked like," Jon replied. "If you were to read the Bible, you would get to know His character and be able to recognize Him."

She lowered her eyebrows in thought. "Well … yeah … I guess you can't recognize something if you don't know what to look for," she reasoned. "I never really thought of it like that."

"Yielding your life over is something people choose to do once they realize that God knows best," Jon said. "I walked away from my religion two years ago because I thought I deserved to have as much fun as my friends. You know what? The last two years of my life have not been fun. Yeah, the first few months were a good time, but the fun wasn't worth the consequences. I lost Chantal. I lost my peace of mind. I let partying become my priority, and it led me down a road of self-destruction. Worst of all, I hurt a lot of people along the way. I learned the hard way that God doesn't want us to sin because He knows it causes pain. He isn't trying to make life boring by giving us rules to live by. He's trying to protect us from unnecessary pain because He loves us."

Marielle stared at Jon blankly, clearly overwhelmed by his monologue.

"Look who still has faith after all," Courtney sang, sounding surprised by Jon's insight. "Thanks for speaking up, Anderson."

⊰※⊱

"Seriously, dude, I think I need to go home and take a nap before Andy's thing tonight," Jason said as he trailed behind Chris through the center of town. "I'm beat. I feel like I'm going to pass out. I haven't eaten anything since breakfast."

"So, go in the sub shop and get something," Chris suggested. "We can stop and eat."

"I left my money at home," Jason replied quickly. "I'd rather just eat at my house and then take a half-hour nap."

"Jay, it's five-thirty," Chris stated, halting in his tracks. "You wouldn't even get home 'til six. You're not going to have time to eat *and* nap. We have to be at the church by seven. I think we should get there early to help out since this thing was our idea."

"Come on, guy," Jason whined. "I haven't eaten since eight o'clock this morning. I only slept for two hours last night. I cleaned Alyssa's entire house before I went to bed. I'm beat. I *need* to go home."

"Yeah, and you also haven't taken any pills since this morning," Chris commented dryly.

Jason's eyes widened with anger. "Dude, I said I haven't slept or eaten. Why are you bringing up drugs?"

Chris shook his head from side to side.

"This is ridiculous!" Jason exclaimed, throwing his arms up in the air. "I'm just tired. We've been walking for hours!"

"So," Chris said with a shrug.

"Well, sorry. I'm not in perfect shape like you, and I can't just run around all day without food or water!" Jason yelled.

"I'm not trying to piss you off. I'm just telling you the truth. You feel like crap because you're addicted to a bunch of crap," Chris stated matter-of-factly.

"I'm prescribed Adderall. You make it sound like I do an abundance of illegal drugs," Jason spat, placing his arms across his chest. "I just want to take a nap!"

"Just because you're prescribed something doesn't mean you're not addicted to it," Chris stated sternly. "That's how Taylor got messed up. He got injured on the field, and the doctors prescribed him painkillers. Once he picked up that first bottle, he never picked up another football. You have no idea how messed up his life is right now! You think I'm a good athlete? You should have seen what Taylor was like at our age."

Jason rolled his eyes. "You cannot even compare me to your cousin! He was blowing rails of coke way before he got into oxy. I can't believe you just tried to play that card. I am nothing like Taylor."

Chris sighed. "How can you expect to see things clearly when you're living in the dark?"

Chapter 27

By six thirty the church parking lot was packed so tightly that multiple Montgomery policemen had shown up to direct traffic. The line of cars waiting to turn into the lot extended a mile down Route 108. Luckily, Chris, his mother, his sister Katie, and Jason had arrived at the church around six fifteen—before traffic had grown heavy.

Pastor Mark seemed happy to see Chris and Jason arrive. He gave them booklets to pass out at the doors to the sanctuary. On the booklet's cover was a picture of Andy. Inside was a brief description of the community activities Andy was involved in, awards he had won, information about his family, and scripture from Isaiah 41. The list of community activities took up an entire page.

Jason watched anxiously as crowds of people flooded the sanctuary. As he and Chris handed out the booklets, he noticed how surprised people looked to see them. Whether they were surprised because they didn't associate them with Andy or because they did not expect to see kids with such bad reputations inside a church, it did not make a difference. Jason just smiled and thanked the guests for their support.

"Hello, boys," Chantal greeted them, smiling brightly as she and Alyssa walked into the sanctuary.

"Hey, Tal. Here you go," Jason said and handed her a booklet. "There's a little bit about you in there, you know."

Chantal continued to smile. "I'll save you guys a seat up front with us," she said and winked at the boys before pulling Alyssa toward the front of the room.

A few moments later, Courtney, Bryan, Marielle, and Jon appeared in line for the booklets. They all looked relieved to see Jason and Chris.

"We had no idea what happened to you!" Marielle exclaimed as she took a booklet from Chris. "We thought you might have stayed at Courtney's."

Chris shook his head. "No worries. We covered most of downtown before the stores closed."

Marielle smiled.

"Chantal said she's saving seats up front. Go find her and I'll come sit with you when I'm done," Chris said and gestured toward the altar.

Marielle nodded and followed Courtney down the main aisle.

"Nice job, guy," Bryan stated, patting Jason on the back before following the girls.

Jason nodded in Bryan's direction and then turned to the next guest.

"Hi, guys," Lisa said as she walked up to Chris and Jason a few moments later. Katherine and Leslie were on either side of her. "I can't believe you did all this for Andy. It's so awesome. Thank you for being so strong. We all need it."

"Prayer is powerful," Chris stated and looked at Jason.

Jason nodded and handed each of the girls a booklet.

"Is Cathy here?" Lisa asked, eyeing Jason expectantly.

Jason widened his eyes. He nearly cringed at the sound of his girlfriend's name. "I have no idea," he replied.

Lisa lowered her eyebrows and glanced at him strangely. "Okay … well, we'll see you guys later," she said as she, Katherine, and Leslie entered the sanctuary.

Jason's eyes grew wide when he spotted Cathy's parents and Stephanie making their way toward him.

"Hi, Jason. Hello, Chris," Mrs. Kagelli greeted them with a warm smile. "It's so nice to see you helping out Andy. It means so much to all of us. Andy's family was so touched by the thought. I'm really proud of you both."

"You're good kids," Mr. Kagelli stated while patting Jason on the shoulder.

Jason's jaw dropped slightly before he managed to spread a smile across his face.

By seven o'clock, the boys ran out of the booklets Rachel had printed. Jason and Chris remained at the door, thanking the guests for coming and directing them to the standing-room-only area. Jason's family, Courtney's family, Bobby, Jeff, Adam, and their families, plus Chris's cousin Marc, and Chris's father all arrived slightly after seven. When Andy's father and brother arrived, Jason escorted them to a reserved area by the altar. Mrs. Rosetti had stayed at the hospital, but she sent a message of gratitude.

By seven fifteen, the sanctuary was filled to capacity with people standing practically on top of each other in the aisles. The corridor outside the sanctuary was packed tightly with the overflow. At seven twenty, the worship team began playing on the altar. Jason and Chris quickly made their way to the seats Chantal had saved for them. To Jason's surprise, the music sounded awesome. He had expected depressing organ hymns and a woman singing opera. The worship team sounded like a rock band, and the girl who was singing had the most beautiful voice Jason had ever heard.

"That's Pastor Mark's daughter," Chris whispered to Jason, pointing to the girl with the beautiful voice.

Jason stared intently at the girl. He thought he recognized her from school, but he wasn't positive. The girl he was thinking of had never glanced in his direction. He began wondering if she was single and then quickly halted his thoughts. Someone like her would never want anything to do with someone like him. Just by looking at her, Jason could see there was a special radiance about her. There was life in Pastor Mark's daughter, and it abounded from her like Jason had never seen before. He had not realized how dead he felt until his blue eyes grazed her glowing face.

Jason thought back to when he first met Cathy in seventh grade and the glow he had once seen in her. She had been a lot like Chantal—friendly, considerate, and kind. Remembering that made Jason finally accept that his girlfriend had changed. The limelight had sucked her in, wrung her tightly, and dried the life right out of her.

Chapter 28

Pastor Mark and the four assistant pastors stood on the altar and alternated leading prayer for Andy. They prayed for many different things: that Andy would wake up without mental or physical complications; that God would keep His hand upon Andy; that the doctors and nurses would give Andy the best care possible; that everything that could be done for Andy would be thought of and done; that God would comfort Andy's family and give them His peace that surpasses all understanding; that God would use Andy's circumstance to reach into the hearts of lost souls; that God would give Andy's family the strength needed to get through the days ahead; and that the Kagellis' kitchen would be repaired quickly. Their prayers continued for over an hour. After the pastors concluded, they told everyone to break up into groups and create prayer circles.

Jason, Chris, Chantal, Alyssa, Marielle, Courtney, Bryan, Jon, and Chantal's family formed a circle close to the altar. Marielle, who was holding hands with Courtney and Chris, had her eyes planted on the floor. Bryan, who was standing between Jon and Courtney, was shifting his weight awkwardly from side to side. Jon, who had ended up holding hands with Chantal, was blushing bright red. Alyssa, who was standing between Chantal and her sister Stephanie, kept glancing at Jason. Jason, who was standing between Mr. Kagelli and Chris, was shaking his head sadly at Alyssa. He knew Alyssa was sharing his negative feelings toward Cathy and guessed that most people in the circle were saddened by her absence.

The group bowed their heads as Mr. Kagelli began praying. "Dear Lord," he began, "we come before You, asking You to please deliver Andy safely from a coma. Lord, I know Andy has a great love for You and that all things work together for good for those who love You, so I know You are in complete control of this situation … but I just want to ask You to please spare his life. Please let him awake from a coma without any complications. Please comfort the Rosettis and give them Your peace that surpasses all understanding. I also want to pray for my daughter, Chantal. Please continue to give her strength to get through this with her eyes set on You. Keep her faith strong and bring peace to her broken heart.

"I would also like to lift my daughter, Cathaleen, up to You. Lord, she is so lost, and she is so young. Please place Your hand on her and draw her close to You. Do whatever it takes to bring her back to You," at those words Mr. Kagelli's voice cracked. "Please show her the love You have for her and the love we all have for her. I ask all of this in Jesus' name. Amen."

Jason's eyes had filled with tears while Cathy's father was praying. Cathy was lost, and Jason felt responsible for that. He was the one who introduced her to everything that was destroying her.

Chantal locked eyes with Jason before she began to pray: "Dear Lord, I come before You, asking You to please bring Andy safely out of a coma. I love him so much. I know he can bring great things to this world in Your name. Please spare his life," Chantal pleaded softly as tears plunged from her eyes. "Please comfort the Rosettis and let them know that Andy rests safely in Your care. You bless us so much, and we have so much to be thankful for. Thank you for the friends I have, and for all the support I have been given.

"I ... I want to ask You to place Your hand upon Jason, and comfort him through this. Please show him that none of this is his fault and help him not blame himself for Cathy's behavior. Lord, please draw Jason and my sister close to You. Please keep the devil far away from them so your light can shine through. Please comfort my family. I know they are so worried about Andy and my sister. Please bless Marielle, Courtney, Jason, Chris, Bryan, and Jon for planning this service. It is so cool to see everyone come together for Andy. In Jesus' name I pray, Amen." Chantal released her hand from Alyssa's grip and wiped tears from her saturated face.

"God, we haven't spoken in a long time, and I hope You don't mind listening to me pray, even though I am not a good person like Chantal," Jason stated suddenly, lifting his head toward the ceiling. "I just want to pray for Andy, that he makes it out alive ... and that somehow he feels how much people in Montgomery care about him. We love him, and we're all here because we know we are helpless without You. So, please, God, give Andy the strength to pull through. In the name of the Father, the Son, and the Holy Spirit, Amen." Jason lowered his head and glanced uncomfortably at the floor. He closed his eyes tightly, hoping no one would notice the tears that had once again filled his eyes.

"Lord, I just want to thank You for my best friend Jason," Chris said quietly. "Without him I don't think this prayer service would have happened. Please comfort Chantal, her family, and the Rosettis. Show me how I can help them. More than anything, I want Andy to wake up healthy from a coma. I know You have the power to make that happen. Please give him strength. In Jesus' name I pray, Amen."

"Let's take a few more minutes to finish up our personal prayers, and then I'm going to ask the worship team to come back up on stage," Pastor Mark stated a moment later from the pulpit. "If anyone needs prayer, please come to the altar and see one of the pastors."

Without hesitation, Jon pulled free from the prayer circle and hustled to the altar.

"Chantal, if you want to go up for prayer, I'll go with you," Courtney offered, placing a supportive hand on Chantal's arm.

Chantal smiled appreciatively at Courtney. "That would be nice. Thanks," she said, taking hold of Courtney's outreached hand.

Chapter 29

Following Andy's service, the Kagellis opened their home for fellowship. Cathy, startled by the noise that had erupted throughout her house, rushed downstairs with Julianna. The two girls stood in the foyer, glancing around in disbelief. Cathy lowered her eyebrows, crossed her arms, and pouted.

"Looks like your parents decided to throw a party," Julianna commented quietly.

Cathy rolled her eyes. "Let's get out of here," she said as she began stomping up the stairs. The phone was ringing when the girls entered her room. Cathy hesitated before picking up her cordless phone. She had left Jason five messages that day. It was unlike him to avoid her. "Hello?" she called lifelessly into the phone.

"Where were you tonight?" Lisa's distraught voice exclaimed. "I cannot believe you didn't come pray for Andy. I know you don't like church—I don't either—but seriously, Kagelli, it was for Andy."

Cathy sighed and fell back on her bed. "I got so sick last night from whatever I took, and then I woke up with such a hangover," she responded dramatically. "I thought drinking some wine would revive me, but instead it knocked me out."

"Big surprise," Lisa commented sarcastically. "Leslie is sleeping over. Do you want to come over, too? I heard your parents invite the whole church back to your house, so I figured you'd want to get out of there."

Cathy laughed. "My parents are insane. There's like fifty people downstairs. Oh, and guess who is in the midst of all the church people?"

"Jason?" Lisa guessed.

"No. He's MIA," Cathy replied without much emotion. "Alyssa! Alyssa's downstairs right now, hanging out with Chantal, Courtney, and all of their loser friends. It's hilarious. I guess she doesn't want to be popular anymore—just like Chris. Remember when Chris was the most popular boy in our grade?"

"Chris is still cool. He's just different now," Lisa stated matter-of-factly. "I'm almost afraid to talk to him. I look like a murderer next to him."

Cathy laughed. "Um, yeah, I don't get it. He used to be awesome. Seriously, he was so much fun. I hope he snaps out of the trance he's in. Jay's so annoying without Chris around."

"They were inseparable all day," Lisa said. "I thought if they hung out, Jay would corrupt Chris back into his old ways, but it looked to me like Chris was rubbing off on Jay. Your boyfriend volunteered at the service tonight; he handed everyone booklets about Andy."

"What?" Cathy laughed. "You have got to be kidding me. Jason would never do that! He doesn't even like Andy!"

"Yeah. It was pretty weird to see. Jay and Chris were manning the door and helping people find seats. They seemed really into the whole prayer thing," Lisa explained.

Cathy widened her eyes. "What is wrong with everyone today? I cannot believe my boyfriend would do something like that. I thought Julianna was kidding when she said the prayer service was his idea."

"What is up with you hanging out with that girl?" Lisa questioned her in a disapproving tone.

"Julianna's right here," Cathy said politely. "Do you want to say hi?"

Lisa laughed. "You are terrible. Whatever. You can both come here if you want. It would be cool to have the company. You know how to take my mind off things. I really can't believe something so terrible happened to someone so incredible."

"Incredible? Andy's all right," Cathy sang. "I'll refrain from my true feelings because he is your best friend and currently not doing so hot. Can your brother pick us up? We'll come over, but I feel like crap and don't want to walk."

"Let me go ask," Lisa said and abruptly ended the call.

"Julianna, call your mother and ask if you can sleep over my house tonight," Cathy stated while handing Julianna the phone. "Tell her my parents invited everyone back after the service and you want to stay here."

"Aren't we going somewhere?" Julianna asked.

Cathy rolled her eyes. "Yeah, but I doubt your mom would let you sleep over Lisa's. Don't tell her. Everyone knows that Lisa doesn't have parents."

Julianna stared at Cathy for a moment, pondering her response. One week prior, Julianna thought she would never get a chance to hang out with Cathy or Lisa. Cathy, Lisa, Leslie, Katherine, and Alyssa were the most popular girls in her grade. Julianna did not believe she had the looks, the social skills, or the reputation to associate with any of them. She just wanted to feel like she belonged somewhere.

When high school first began, Courtney had broken Julianna's heart by disregarding their decade-long friendship. She had never felt so abandoned and worthless. Then Jon entered

Julianna's life and offered her hope. He rescued her from the despair and self-pity she had been indulging in. He made her feel valuable. Earlier that week, she had been so thankful for him. Why had she dismissed him so callously? What had made her say such accusatory things to him?

Thinking about Jon made Julianna's head spin. She had come to a crossroads and needed to pick a route. If she went to Lisa's instead of apologizing to Jon downstairs, she knew there would be no turning back. The biggest question boggling her mind was who did she want to be? She felt like a wave in the sea, constantly being tossed around by the changing forces of the wind.

Chapter 30

"Chantal, I'm really sorry to hear about Andy," Marc Dunkin said as he took a seat beside Chantal on her living room couch. "I talked to Robby Rosetti, and he's a mess about the whole thing. I can only imagine how you must feel right now."

"Thanks for coming here," Chantal said, smiling widely. "I think it's really sweet of you, considering how I never talked to you after that night at Chris's. I'm sorry about that. I just got confused." She looked around at her friends, realizing she probably should not have spoken so loudly. While her boyfriend was in a coma, she had no business expressing her emotions to a hot senior.

Marc shrugged and spread his full lips into a smirk. "Hey, I'm not going to hold anything against you."

Chantal smiled appreciatively at Marc and felt her cheeks begin to redden. Suddenly, butterflies began fluttering around in her stomach, and she remembered why she had avoided him in the first place. Just by sitting near her, Marc gave her body a physical reaction that she could not explain.

"Tal, are you talking about the night of Jay's party? When we were at Chris's?" Jon piped in, glancing disapprovingly at Chantal. "Or did you guys hang out another time?"

Chantal widened her eyes. "No, it was just that night!" she exclaimed.

"Oh, I was just wondering because I didn't realize you two really even knew each other," Jon said and gazed uneasily at Chantal.

Chantal shot Jon a questioning glance. Maybe Alyssa had been right? Maybe Jon did still like her? For whatever the reason, Jon seemed disturbed by Chantal and Marc's short conversation.

"Well, maybe if she had returned my calls, I'd know her a little better," Marc laughed.

Chantal had begun to admire the light blue shade of Marc's eyes, when Jon suddenly stormed across the room. Whipping her head around, Chantal noticed Cathy and Julianna standing by the front door. The sight of Cathy brought sadness upon her heart. As Chantal watched Cathy and Julianna slip seemingly unnoticed out the door, she began silently praying for them. She didn't know Julianna very well, but she knew hanging out with Cathy would do nothing but corrupt her.

Chantal turned back around to face Marc.

He was staring at her with a puzzled expression. "Did I say something to upset Anderson?" he asked, raising his eyebrows.

Chantal shook her head and rolled her eyes. "I don't think so. His ex-girlfriend just walked out the door with my sister. They just broke up the other day, so I think the sight of her upset him."

"Oh, wait, that girl he showed up with at Chris's? That little quiet girl?" Marc asked.

Chantal nodded. "Yeah, Julianna. She's decided to take a sip of my sister's world—something Jon wants nothing to do with. He knows what it's like to hang out with my sister."

"Yeah, I know Cathy," Marc said in an uneasy tone. "You two don't seem anything alike."

"Well, we were best friends before she dated Jason. She's changed a lot in the last couple of years."

"Yeah, but you know Jay is a good kid," Marc said. "He has too much going for him to waste his life partying. He'll snap out of it quickly—just like Chris did," he commented, nodding toward his younger cousin who was standing by the fireplace with Marielle.

"Chris only snapped out of it because he found God," Chantal stated. "He's the first to admit that he couldn't get sober on his own. Do you think Jason will actually straighten out? I think he's a really nice kid, but he's got some problems."

"Eh," Marc said and leaned his head in thought, "who knows? Maybe he will. Maybe he won't. He's not as deep into stuff as Chris was, so he has a better chance. It's a lot easier to give up drinking and smoking than the stuff Chris was doing."

"Jason doesn't smoke," Chantal corrected him. "Well, he smokes a lot of weed but not cigarettes."

"No, I know that," Marc said. "I meant weed. Weed's more mentally addictive than physically addictive, so it's not like he would need detox. I don't really know what else he's done, but as long as he's kept his nose and veins free of opiates, he has a good chance of straightening out."

"I don't know what he's done either," Chantal said. "I don't even know the full extent of what Chris was into. I just pray for them both. Seeing the way Jay was in church tonight made me smile. I think there's a chance he'll straighten out. At least he has Chris's example to follow. I think the change in Chris has inspired a lot of people. Not that Chris was ever a bad person, but a lot of people thought he was headed in a bad direction."

"Yeah, I know," Marc said. "I think my brothers are to blame for that mess. You want to talk about corrupt? You should see my brother Taylor. He's a mess. I can't believe my aunt and uncle leave him in charge of Katie and Chris. That's like leaving a baby in a den of lions."

"Why, what's wrong with your brother?" Chantal questioned Marc, lowering her eyebrows.

Marc shrugged. "Last year, he got hurt playing football and had to take the rest of the season off. After that, he lost all athletic and academic motivation. He ended up losing his scholarship and failing out of his major."

"Holy crap!" Chantal exclaimed, widening her eyes. "Taylor's a football legend. Why did he just give up like that?"

Marc let out a heavy breath. "Well, he got hurt pretty badly and had to have two surgeries on his knee. The doctor put him on painkillers ... he was really depressed about not playing football ... one thing led to another ... it's a really long story. Basically, he medicated his pain and depression with drugs—stronger ones than the doctor ordered—and became an addict. I mean, he always partied before—everyone in Montgomery knew Taylor was a complete animal—but the stuff he's doing now is ruining him."

"Wow. That's a really sad story," Chantal said, eyeing Marc sympathetically.

"Yeah, it is," Marc stated matter-of-factly. "I don't even know how to help him. I tried to get him to go to detox, but he wanted no part of it. My parents are still mourning the loss of his scholarship and football career. They have no idea that he has a drug problem; they think he's just depressed. My brother Jordan is playing ball for Notre Dame, so he's not around to help—not that he'd be much help anyway ... sorry, I don't really get along with Jordan. Anyway, Chris and I are Taylor's only hope. I've never had a drug problem, so I can't relate to him, but Chris can. Once Chris gets a little stronger in his sobriety, I'm going to bring him to see Taylor. Taylor knows how messed up Chris used to be, so maybe the change in Chris will get his attention."

"That's a good idea," Chantal commented. "I'm sure Chris would love to help him."

"Oh, he definitely would," Marc agreed. "I just can't bring Chris around Taylor until I know for sure that it won't cause Chris to stumble. In fact, I told my aunt and uncle not to let Taylor housesit the next time they go away. Chris really needs to stay away from drugs and alcohol. Now that he's sober, he wants to help other people get sober, but he has to be really careful. After only two months of sobriety, he could relapse in a second."

"That's an awful thought," Chantal said, glancing across the room at Chris. "He's doing so well."

"It's an awful thought but a harsh reality," Marc said. "As long as he keeps going to church and hanging out with Marielle, you, and Jon, he should be all right."

"Was it bad that he spent the day with Jason?" Chantal asked.

"I'm pretty sure they were focused on Andy's service and didn't have time to get in trouble," Marc reasoned. "But, actually, he shouldn't spend time with Jay. I'll talk to him about that."

"I never realized that staying sober was just as hard as getting sober," Chantal admitted. "I guess I don't know much about recovery."

"I think it's different for each person," Marc said thoughtfully. "The first year of sobriety is rough for everyone. It usually gets a little easier as time goes on. Chris is in a battle right now—but he knows it. It's great that he has football, straightedge friends, and his newfound faith to keep him busy. He has looked into joining a teen recovery program as well. He's doing all the right things."

"You know so much about this stuff," Chantal said, shaking her head. "How?"

"My dad is a recovered alcoholic," Marc replied. "He's been sober for fifteen years. I used to go to Al-Anon meetings with my mom all the time."

"Oh, wow," Chantal said. "Did Taylor ever go to those meetings?"

Marc nodded.

"Oh. Well, I guess he didn't take them as seriously as you did," Chantal concluded. "I'm really sorry to hear that he's not doing well. I can kind of relate to how you must feel. I don't think Cathy's doing very well. She worries me."

"Isn't that funny? It's like we were meant to have this conversation or something," Marc laughed. "I'm so comfortable talking to you. Usually I don't talk this openly about my family."

"Oh, I do!" Chantal laughed and then smiled at Marc. "I mean, I like to talk, but I'm not usually this comfortable with someone I've only hung out with once before."

Marc smiled back at Chantal. "Well, I'd really like to talk to you again sometime. Not to hit on you or anything but just to talk about this stuff. I hope I didn't scare you when I called you before."

Chantal beamed. "You didn't scare me at all. Actually, talking to you tonight has really lifted my spirits."

"Yes!" Marc exclaimed, pumping his fist in the air. "That's what I was aiming for."

Chantal laughed and rolled her eyes. "You're a nut."

Chapter 31

Jason remained completely silent during the drive home from Andy's service. He stared aimlessly out the tinted window of his father's black Cadillac Escalade as his mind danced around in circles. It was hyperactively getting him nowhere. He knew he couldn't avoid Cathy or her phone calls forever—although, he liked entertaining that thought.

As Jason reflected on his day, he realized it had been one of the most productive days of his life. Chris, Jon, Marielle, Courtney, and Bryan were not even close with Andy, yet they had happily devoted their entire day to his cause. Unlike Jason, they felt zero-percent responsible for Andy's accident, yet they put just as much effort forth as he had. Cathy, who should have felt somewhat responsible, had done nothing to support anyone beside herself.

Jason stared his translucent blue eyes blankly out the window, gazing at home after home, wondering how he could date someone so inconsiderate. He had once had good friends. Spending one day with his old friends, and one day without Cathy, had been the perfect antidote for Jason's depression.

Jason had always thought of Cathy as "the drug" that made him feel best about himself; she was attractive, popular, funny, adventurous, and a trophy to proudly show off to his friends. He had never thought much about why hanging out with her made him feel better; he had accepted it at face value. During the prayer service, he had had a revelation. Lately, Cathy had been acting just enough crueler, more untamed, and more reckless than Jason to make him feel responsible, kind, and compassionate. Jason didn't have to feel bad about his lifestyle when his girlfriend was beside him acting even more immoral.

By surrounding himself with people wilder than him, Jason had been able to live in complete darkness. There had never been a threat of light shining on him, exposing his own devious nature. There had been no need to feel convicted when everyone around him was doing the same things. Those "things" were what Jason had thought would bring him happiness. After spending one day with Chris, Jason had begun to question every aspect of that theory.

Jason and Chris had met in kindergarten and had grown up inseparable. Chris had accompanied the Davids on at least half of their family vacations. Jason and Chris had been Cub Scouts together and on the same sports teams year after year. In fifth grade, Chris had asked Jason's first girlfriend out for him, and Jason had done the same for Chris. They had snuck into their first R-rated movie together, and then into Mr. Dunkin's liquor cabinet a year later. Jason smiled at the thought of all the stunts they had pulled together. For a decade, Jason and Chris had been partners in crime. Then one day, without warning, their adventure came to a crashing halt.

Jason had always enjoyed Chris's company more than anyone's. Two months without his best friend had felt indescribably long and depressing. Passing by the "new Chris" in school had turned Jason's stomach numerous times. He had resented Chris for turning his back on their friendship. Instead of trying to understand why Chris had distanced himself, Jason had indulged in drugs to keep his mind off the situation.

A month later, Jason's body ached, he had developed insomnia, the void had not been filled, and he was emotionally shot. Partying on the weekends was one thing; trying to get through every day in a daze was a completely different story. Inducing himself with drugs had gotten Jason nowhere good, very quickly.

Without ceasing, Jason had made fun of Chris for turning his life around. He had even trash-talked Chris to Bryan and Jon. The only person Jason hadn't badmouthed Chris to was Chris, because Jason didn't actually believe any of the terrible things he was saying. Chris was fully aware of the rumors Jason had spread about him and the damage Jason had brought to his reputation. *Who in their right mind gives up the social limelight for a life of sobriety?* Jason hadn't been able to make sense of it until he spent some time with "new Chris"—the Chris who lent Jason an ear, despite every slanderous thing Jason had said about him.

Jason knew Chris better than anyone did. He had been there for all the highs and lows of his life. While Andy was in a coma, and everyone was falling apart around him, Chris radiated with strength. Jason knew Chris cared about Andy just as much as everyone else did, but somehow Chris had been able to find peace with the situation. Jason had never seen Chris act so secure or consoling.

What completely blew Jason's mind was the newfound strength he saw in his best friend. Chris had a lot of family problems, which had left him quite broken. He had dealt with issues of abandonment and discouragement his entire life. Chris had always been weak to temptation and reluctant to step up to plate. Having an abundance of friends and a fun idea always up his sleeve, he had managed to keep most people from noticing the deep scars of his life.

Jason's mind continued to wander. He thought about the different people he had come in contact with that day. Many of them had left an impact on him. He remembered how shocked he had been by Mr. Kagelli's kind words; he had called Jason a good kid. How

Cathy's father managed to see any good in Jason was a mystery to him.

Next, Jason thought of the secretary at the church, Rachel, and the kindness that had radiated from her. The warmth of her personality had amazed Jason. He realized Chris had a lot in common with Mr. Kagelli and Rachel. Then Jason thought of Pastor Mark. His words had been running through Jason's mind since their discussion.

Without any intention of doing so, Jason had ended up baring his soul to the pastor. He had confessed everything from having premarital sex to being addicted to Adderall. Tears had plunged from his eyes when he had told Pastor Mark how he had treated Chris. Their entire conversation had been a huge cry for help on Jason's part. At one point, everything in his life had seemed like fun and games; then, without warning, it had turned into a death sentence.

After forty-five minutes of rambling, Jason had told Pastor Mark that he felt lifeless. Pastor Mark said that he should feel dead inside because his spirit was dead.

"Everyone's spirit—the part of a human that connects with God—is dead until it becomes reborn through Christ," Pastor Mark had said. "Humans are made up of flesh, spirit, and soul. Everyone is born with a living flesh and soul, but the spirit needs to be brought back to life. When Adam and Eve sinned against God in the Garden of Eden, they died a spiritual death. From that moment on, human beings were marred with sin natures. Sin caused the spirit to die because sin creates a barrier between man and God. The word religion means re-link. It means how man is linked back to God. We become re-linked to God and our spirits get revived when the sin barrier between God and us gets wiped away. Jesus bridged the gap between man and God by paying the penalty for all the sins of humanity. He is the link."

Pastor Mark had then told Jason some of his own testimony and how God had delivered him from his own death sentence. He had said, "If God managed to cleanse me of my addictions, anger problem, and foul mouth, God can purify anyone." Pastor Mark had told Jason that he found his faith through one of his high school teachers. Instead of giving him detention on a weekly basis, as most of his teachers had, that particular teacher had taken the time to counsel him. Pastor Mark had told Jason that what he remembered most clearly about his teacher was the undeniable concern and enthusiasm that had radiated from her. He said that after spending only a short amount of time speaking with her, he realized there was something missing from his own life. Instead of reprimanding or psychoanalyzing him, she had explained the love of Christ to him. Pastor Mark admitted, "I was more than skeptical but unable to deny the light that shone from her."

"So, you straightened out your act by asking God to help you do it?" Jason had asked. "It was as simple as that?"

Pastor Mark's answer had surprised Jason. "No. Actually, I asked Him into my life and His Spirit into my heart. He already knew my weaknesses, and He gave me strength when I turned my life over to Him. The strength was a wonderful blessing, but even greater was the gift He gave me. His grace fell upon me, and I was forgiven for all my sins. All of the sex, lies, swears, drunken nights, drugs, and the rest of my sins were wiped clean from my slate. The sin barrier was removed. I was re-linked to my Creator. When I accepted Jesus as my Savior, I was given the gift of eternal life. That day marked the start of my relationship with the Lord; it's the best relationship I have ever been a part of."

At that time, Jason had not been able to put two and two together. The light Pastor Mark had spoken of was the same light Jason had observed shining from Pastor Mark's daughter. At the time of his talk with Pastor Mark, Jason had been reluctant to believe in such a light; now, he could no longer deny the existence of it.

Pastor Mark had made it sound easy to turn away from the fun lifestyle Jason led. The idea of spending time at church events made him cringe. He could not understand how anyone enjoyed living that way, but at the same time, he noticed that the people who did were the happiest people he knew. Being an analytical person, Jason realized he must have missed something.

Pastor Mark had offered Jason the gift of salvation, but Jason had declined, saying he was not ready to accept it. Thinking about it in retrospect, Jason realized he had been foolish not to accept a free gift. Something inside him had told him it was a much bigger commitment. *What about penance and confession? How can God just forgive you for being a horrible person, just because you believe in Jesus? How could anyone love a sinner so much?* Jason realized he could not answer any of his questions because he remembered nothing about the Bible—despite the eight years he had studied at St. Timothy's.

He recalled how at age six he had begged his parents to enroll him in St. Timothy's. He remembered that he had been eager to learn about God. He had completely forgotten about his childhood interest in the Catechism. How had he blocked that out? He sat for a moment, trying to remember what had changed his mind about Catholicism. His eyes grew wide as he remembered the way Luke had teased him, saying that he was going to get molested by a priest. That had filled Jason with all the fear he needed to distance himself from church involvement. He had completely blocked that out of his memory for years.

After his zeal for God had been quenched, he had decided believing in God would be sufficient. It had never dawned on him to get to know God personally. Actually, he had not even realized it was possible to develop the type of relationship with God that Pastor Mark had described: not only having head knowledge of God, but also having experiences with Him. Jason wondered if that was what he had been craving as a child. With his mind dancing back and forth between Pastor Mark, Chris, and Pastor Mark's beautiful daughter, Jason realized they had something he desired.

Once upon a time, Jason had thought he knew the secret to a fulfilling life. He was realizing that he had only been fed the lies of the world. Sex, drugs, a pretty girlfriend, good grades, rich parents, good looks, popularity, and all the other things people believed brought fulfillment, had brought him nothing of the sort.

When Jason arrived home that evening, he locked himself inside his bedroom. He took a seat at his desk and glanced at a framed picture of Cathy and him. They had been on a hike with Chantal and Jon when Chantal had snapped the picture. As Jason gazed steadily at the photo, he was reminded of the hope he had felt on that hike. He remembered the butterflies that had fluttered around in his stomach every time Cathy had smiled, and the sparkle in her eyes he had found so attractive. Sitting at his desk, he remembered how sweet the girl he fell in love with had once been.

Even during his moment of reminisce, Jason knew that picture he treasured so much was filled with the false hope of all the other lies of the world—lies that he had willingly swallowed. For Jason, lies had always been easy to chew up, spit out, and swallow. He would have rather accepted a lie, without any consideration, than put forth the effort to seek the truth. Even when he had accidentally stumbled across the truth, he had closed his eyes, blocked his ears, and slipped into denial.

After letting out a loud sigh, Jason reached across his desk and dropped the picture of him and Cathy facedown onto his desktop. He sat for a moment, with his hands folded, staring at his desk's lamp. Next, he pushed back his chair and reached down to the bottom right drawer. Gliding the drawer open with ease, Jason began shuffling through notebooks, pencils, bags of marijuana, vitamin bottles, loose wads of money, band-aids, and every other random thing that filled his drawer. At the very bottom, he found exactly what he was looking for and brought it to his mahogany desktop.

"John," he said aloud, and rolled his chair closer to his desk. He swallowed deeply and opened the book he had retrieved from his drawer. He looked down and slowly turned the pages until he saw the name he had spoken in the upper right-hand corner. His eyes traveled down the page and rested at the large number one. Jason's eyes grew wide as they moved from left to right across the page:

"In the beginning was the Word, and the Word was with God, and the Word was God. He was in the beginning with God. All things were made through Him; and without Him nothing was made that was made. **In Him was life, and the life was the light of men. And the light shines in the darkness, and the darkness did not comprehend it."**

Other Books

By Stacy A. Padula

Gripped Part 1: The Truth We Never Told

In high school, Taylor Dunkin broke more records than any other athlete to step foot in Montgomery, Massachusetts. As a sophomore in college, he was ranked by ESPN as one of the NFL's top 100 prospects. However, his aspirations came to a jarring halt when a season-ending injury sent him spiraling into a dark world of pain, depression, and addiction.

One year later, Taylor is a person of interest in a highly confidential investigation headed by the Boston Police Department. He has entangled himself in a crime ring notorious for pushing drugs on local college campuses. Montgomery's hometown hero has fallen hard, and he's taking a lot of people down with him.

Luke Davids has become the middleman between Taylor and teens in Montgomery who want to buy drugs. Freshmen Cathy Kagelli, Chris Dunkin, and Jason Davids are just a few of the students at Montgomery Lake High who have fallen victim to the benzos and opiates supplied by Taylor and Luke.

When Taylor's youngest brother Marc discovers that Taylor is behind the copious amount of pills circulating around his high school, he sets off to not only reverse the damage Taylor has caused, but also save his lifelong role model from becoming a casualty of America's deadly opioid epidemic.

Gripped Part 2: Blindsided

Fourteen-year-old Chris Dunkin is known for being the life of the party and everyone's favorite friend. Despite his amicable nature, he carries around deep-seated pain from his childhood that he frequently numbs with alcohol and drugs.

After hosting a party, Chris awakes with a strange vibe running through his body and no recollection of the previous night. When he learns the horrifying truth of what his night entailed, the trajectory of his life is changed forever.

Gripped Part 3: The Fallout

After a near-death experience, Chris Dunkin begins surrounding himself with positive influences and putting his efforts towards living a clean lifestyle. However, the night before school starts, his best friend Jason convinces him to host a party that shows Chris more about himself than he actually wants to know.

Meanwhile, Marc Dunkin has received word from a detective that his oldest brother Taylor is a person of interest in a highly confidential case headed by the Boston Police Department. They know Taylor's clean; they know he wants out of the game; and they want to help make that happen. However, their "help" will come at a cost—one that may put Taylor and his entire family in grave danger. Taylor is trying to get his life back in order after an opiate addiction wreaked havoc on his once promising athletic future. Getting clean was a difficult feat, but breaking free from the Bilotti crime ring will present an even greater challenge.

Gripped Part 4: Smoke & Mirrors

After spending her first month of high school grounded, Cathy Kagelli is finally allowed to socialize and uncover what her boyfriend, Jason Davids, has been up to without her. When Cathy realizes Jason has been experimenting with a variety of drugs, she devises a plan to save him from himself... but she just may lose herself in the process.

Meanwhile Taylor Dunkin finds himself playing a game with even higher stakes because his life, his reputation, and the safety of everyone he loves are all on the line. Taylor's two younger brothers, Jordan and Marc, have been at odds for years, but they are brought together to decipher the mysterious clues Taylor is leaving regarding his whereabouts. As secrets are revealed, the Dunkin boys' relationships will be changed forever. In Taylor's weakest moment, he made a deal with the devil, and now there is a reckoning. But who will pay the price?

Gripped Part 5: Taylor's Story

Taylor Dunkin is missing.

The last message Jordan Dunkin receives from Taylor leads him to Taylor's abandoned Jeep. Each of Taylor's family members holds a piece of the puzzle, and as the Dunkins begin putting the details together, they are awakened to the possibility they may never see Taylor again.

No one can find Missy Kent.

Missy's boyfriend Luke Davids last saw her dancing with their friends at a nightclub, but she hasn't responded to anyone's texts or calls for hours.

Everything is connected.

Taylor and Missy's friends are dangerously close to learning the truth, but their ignorance might be the only thing keeping them safe. Every clue is leading them closer to peril.

The fifth book in the Gripped series moves through details at a thrilling pace. Secrets are revealed and lives are at stake. Taylor, Missy, their friends, and their families must figure out who they can trust before it's too late.

Montgomery Lake High #1: The Right Person

Growing up in the shadow of two NFL-destined cousins, Chris Dunkin has high hopes for his own future in football. However, a drug addiction threatens to destroy everything he has worked hard to attain. When Chris meets Courtney Angeletti—the mayor's straightedge Christian daughter—he believes she could be the source of inspiration he needs to overcome his destructive lifestyle. Courtney, however, has other ideas.

The desire to rebel has been tugging on Courtney's heartstrings for some time, and Chris's "bad-boy" reputation draws her to him like a moth to a flame. After all, he is a central part of the most popular clique in her high school. Will Chris pull Courtney away from her faith or will Courtney inspire him to overcome his rebellious lifestyle?

Montgomery Lake High #3: The Aftermath

At age fifteen, Jason Davids appears to have it all: high grades, popular friends, a beautiful girlfriend, and nearly any worldly thing that promises enjoyment at his disposal. Despite this, there is a persistent emptiness inside his heart. After failing to fill the void with achievements, relationships, and illicit substances, Jason finds himself intrigued by Jessie: a rather quiet girl, who is the daughter of a local pastor. How is it possible that she stands for everything his lifestyle opposes yet possesses the one thing he has been searching for all along?

Montgomery Lake High #4: The Battle for Innocence

Jon Anderson and Chantal Kagelli are trying to live moral lives, but temptations are plaguing them in and out of school. Will they continue to be lights in their best friends' lives or will they get pulled into the darkness?

Montgomery Lake High #5: The Forces Within

After being trapped inside his own body, unable to communicate with anyone but his own thoughts, Andy Rosetti finally wakes up from the coma that controlled his life for one month. But upon awakening, Andy finds himself and his friends in an unfamiliar setting: a mansion riddled with secret passages and supernatural forces. As his friends fall prey to the entities surrounding them, Andy must figure out if the darkness lies within the mansion's walls or within the people surrounding him.

About the Author

Stacy Padula grew up in Pembroke, Massachusetts. She is the founder of Briley & Baxter Publications, the founder of South Shore College Consulting & Tutoring, a co-founder of BLE Pictures, and the author of thirteen books. She began writing her first book series, *Montgomery Lake High*, when she was a teenager because she saw a need for realistic Y.A. books that address topics such as substance abuse and bullying. Between 2010-2014 all five *Montgomery Lake High* books were published. In 2017, she began writing her second series, *Gripped*, which serves as both a prequel and sequel to her first series. *Gripped* parts 1-5 were published between 2019-2021. She is currently writing part 6. In 2019, she also wrote her first screenplay, an adaptation of her novel *The Aftermath*, and worked on writing a pilot for *Gripped*, which caught the attention of Hollywood producers.

In 2020, she began writing a third book series with NBA Coach Brett Gunning. Geared towards children ages three through eight, Stacy and Brett's *On The Right Path* book series has been endorsed by Joel Osteen, Mike D'Antoni, and Kevin McHale as a series that belongs in every school, library, and household. Both Stacy's Gripped series and On the Right Path series are currently being adapted for TV by Emmy award-winning producer Mark Blutman.

Stacy has been featured in Marquis Who's Who in America (2018-Present) for excellence in literature and education, Marquis Who's Who in the World (2018-Present), and Cambridge Who's Who for Young Professionals (2009). In 2018, she was awarded the Albert Nelson Lifetime Achievement Award, and in 2019, the International Association of Top Professionals (IAOTP of New York, NY) chose Stacy as its "Top Educational Consultant of the Year."

In 2020, she was named "Empowered Woman of the Year" by IAOTP and a "Social Impact Hero" by Authority Magazine for her support of animal rescues through her publishing company. She was also chosen to be on the cover of T.I.P. Magazine, an international business publication.

In June of 2021, Stacy was featured on the famous Reuters Building in Times Square as Empowered Woman of the Year. In 2022, she was named "Top Inspirational Author of the Year" and was honored at a gala at the Bellagio in Las Vegas in December. She was also broadcast for her award on the Planet Hollywood Jumbotron overlooking the Las Vegas Strip. Her novel *Gripped Part 5: Taylor's Story* won the Silver Award and *Gripped Part 1: The Truth We Never Told* won the Gold Award for "Best Teen Book" in the 2022 Readers' Choice Awards.

For 2023, Stacy has been named "Top Global Impact Author of the Year" for her literary work on several continents, and she will be honored at a gala at The Plaza in New York City. In addition, she was chosen to be featured in an international publication titled 50 Fearless Leaders for 2023. She also was asked to serve as a judge for the Scholastic Art & Writing Awards, the nation's oldest and most prestigious contest for creative young adults, sponsored by Bloomberg Philanthropies, The New York Times, and Scholastic.

Connect with Us!

Gripped Book Series Instagram @gripped.book.series
Stacy's Instagram @author_stacypadula
Stacy's Twitter @MLHBookSeries
Cathy's Instagram @ckagelli99
Chantal's Instagram @chantal_kagelli
Jason's Instagram @jds_on
Lisa's Instagram @lisa_ankerman99
Chris's Instagram @dunkin_85
Luke's Instagram @lukedavids97
Alyssa's Instagram @alyssa_kelly02
www.stacyapadula.com
www.brileybaxterbooks.com
www.highambition.org

Did You Enjoy MLH #2?

If you loved this book, would you leave a review on Amazon?